A Switch In Time

The President Is Missing

By

Casi McLean

&

Eleanor LaRue

"USA Today Bestselling Author, Casi McLean, takes us on a journey through the underbelly of society ripped from today's headlines in this
fascinating time travel suspense."

A Switch in Time

ISBN Number: 9798747667662

Based on the manuscript *A Matter Of Principle* by Eleanor LaRue

Contact Information: casi@casimclean.com

Cover Art by the amazing Ada Frost

Editing and Proofreading by N.N. Light

Published in the United States of America

DEDICATION

To my mother, Eleanor LaRue, whose vision
reached far beyond her time.

A part of her lives on in my heart,

and her love, support, and creativity shines through

in everything I do…and everything I am.

.

Praise For Casi McLean

Love the premise of this novel—Serenity
This is a powerfully written and poignant story which will captivate the attention of the readers. So glad that this author took her Mom's manuscript and followed through. The premise is as solid as it was in the 1960's when Eleanor LaRue penned it. Most highly recommended.

Highly Recommend—Enrico Grafitti
This is a solid tale with an outstanding moral theme that I would even suggest be read, and discussed at length, in all modern educational institutions in the hope its lessons are ingrained into the very souls of future generations. Highly recommended.

Social Injustice with a Time Travel Twist—
Jannine Gallant   Originally written in the 60s by Ms. McLean's mother, this story gives a gritty perspective on race relations from that period in American history that is extremely relevant now. The author updates the story with a time travel element. I was drawn into this narrative, hoping the characters would learn and grow. Casi McLean doesn't disappoint!

A Timely Novel Applicable to Today's Turmoil—
Aaron Lazar   A Switch in Time is a timely novel primarily set in 1960, but completely applicable to today's turmoil and racial unrest. Written by Casi McLean based on a manuscript written in 1960 by Eleanor LaRue, her mother, the combined talents of mother and daughter shine with the light of sensitivity and understanding, while keeping the reader on the edge of his/her proverbial seat. Eleanor died in 1995, bequeathing the manuscript to her daughter, who had not yet started to write her excellent stable of novels. Thank you, Casi and Eleanor, for a work that brings great

delight as well as depth of the human condition to our shelves.

This book needs to be read by every world citizen of every race—N.N. Light   A Switch in Time is a compelling thriller ripped from today's headlines. What's ironic about my statement is that this book was written by Casi's mother in the late 1960's. Racial injustice, whether it happens in the 1960's or today, is not only relevant but life-changing. The time has come for all citizens to stand up and say we're in this together. The authors weave an adrenaline-boosting thriller with an important message. The characters are so well-drawn, I was sucked right in. I whipped through the pages faster than my fingers would allow. Emory and James are at the heart of this story and their relationship from mortal enemies to friends is heart-wrenching. The plot moves at a fast pace and there is plenty of action to please any thriller reader. One of the best books I've read this year. It needs to be read by every world citizen of every race. Highly recommend!

A Tour de Force!—Kindle Customer   What an insightful, riveting, and touching time travel story, packed with vivid descriptions, a realistic look at race relations, and ultimately, the need for trust. Beautifully written, this is a book to savor. Highly recommend.

Acknowledgements

I'd like to extend my special thanks to my critique partners, Lori Powers and Linda Carroll-Bradd and to my beta readers, Kathi Goldwyn and Mary Schiller.

I'm forever thankful for the friendship and support or all my readers. You are my inspiration.

A Note To My Readers

As my mother, Eleanor LaRue, and I wrote this this novel—sixty years apart—we scripted the text to allow readers to experience the reality of society and its effect on individuals through the eyes of our characters. What readers take away from the story will be reliant upon the depth and shallowness of each individual.

—Casi McLean

Perhaps John Steinbeck expressed the thought more clearly in Grapes of Wrath:

"Throughout, I've tried to make the reader participate in the actuality,

what he takes from it will be scaled on his own depth and shallowness.
There are five layers in this book, a reader will find as many as he can

and [no] more than he has in himself."

~ John Steinbeck, ~

The Grapes of Wrath

A Switch In Time

The President Is Missing . . .

"Those who control the present, control the past and

those who control the past, control the future.

George Orwell's—1984"

Epilogue

Present Day

E mery Clayton peered through a dusty windowpane unnoticed from the grounds below. He could almost hear the whispers of those who strode before him. Hidden behind storage closets and nestled beneath the sloped ceiling on the north side of the White House, this secluded attic chamber offered the president a secret refuge to escape the bustling activity of the halls below. Emery might never have found the room himself, had he not searched for a quiet spot away from the madding crowd.

For the last three years, he found solace within

this secret space…a place to think and sort through the dissidence running rampant in the America he so dearly loved. As President, he straddled the pinnacle of a double-edged sword threatening the fabric of the nation's democracy.

Dropping his gaze, he turned and paced toward an old wooden secretary. No longer did the Resolute Desk sit with pride in the Oval Office. Cast aside in a forgotten room by his predecessors, the oak treasure, an 1880 gift from Queen Victoria, now gathered dust and cobwebs, a powerless image of a shattered country. Pondering how he'd heal the polarized Congress and divided population paralyzing the nation, he resolved to unite America. Never would he sit idly by and watch this country wither and die.

Emery ran a palm over the smooth surface. His finger touched an etched insignia carved into the wooden drawer. Drawing his glasses from his breast pocket, he perched them on the end of his nose and read aloud the words inscribed.

"God grant me wisdom to light the way and the strength of our forefathers to save the day."

A heartbeat later, President Emery Clayton III vanished into a swirling tempest of blue haze.

Chapter One

In a whirl of nausea, Emery tilted his head backward against his seat and squeezed his eyes shut, eager to temper the sensation. Swallowing hard, he squinted then refocused on his surroundings. No longer did the Resolute Desk lie before him. Instead, a long aisle stretched forward, lined by double seating on either side. Where was he?

Oddly, he recognized his location as the interior of an antique Boeing 707. Something was wrong—very wrong. Was he dreaming? Perhaps he collapsed... or had a stroke. He pinched his forearm, hoping to awaken from the curious dream. Other than a slight twinge of pain... nothing changed. The jet engines roared, causing a burning blaze of fire ants to prickle down his spine, biting... stinging until they gnawed into his stomach.

Nothing about the last few minutes made sense. Beads of sweat formed along his hairline as he reeled possibilities. Perhaps someone tailed him from within the White House and kidnapped him. No. He'd always been careful when he stole away. No one suspected his moments of solitude lured him farther than his personal suite. But something had happened. Maybe someone drugged him... Had he lost consciousness? If so, for how long? Had someone abducted him... thrust him into this inexplicable charade? He scanned the aircraft then peered out the window. No, creating this situation would be impossible... and what benefit would be gained?

Again, he squeezed his eyes and prepared himself for whatever followed. Thoughts spinning, he challenged his memory, but nothing more surfaced beyond a faint recollection... the hidden room in his attic refuge faded, drifted into the distance then vanished into a hazy mist. As President of the United States, he would show no weakness. He'd simply play along while he unraveled the mystery.

A voice blared over the intercom. "We're preparing for take-off. Please fasten your seatbelts."

Utterly confused, Emery fumbled with the clasp to fulfill the request. After repeated attempts, he gave an impatient tug on the right strap caught under the connecting seat. With a thud, the belt loosened.

A glower from the cumbersome woman dressed in vintage clothing overlapping the adjoining seat shriveled his success into an awkward faux pas. She harrumphed then squeezed into the aisle and sat in an empty seat one row ahead. Finally locking the clasp, Emery shrugged and turned toward the window.

Whining jets rumbled into a steady scream as the silver-blue aircraft backed away from the loading ramp and taxied toward the runway. A flight attendant began her spiel, instructing passengers on the use of floatation devices, oxygen masks, and the location of emergency escape hatches. But her attire, circa the nineteen sixties, sent an eerie chill down Emery's back. Noting the antiquity of equipment, he clenched his hands, squeezing the armrests until his fingers numbed.

As the velocity of the take-off held him in place, Emery struggled to grasp where the hell he was. Releasing his grip, he drew his hands to his lap then tapped his fingers on his knee.

Odd memories mingled with his own. Travel plans assigned only a few hours earlier gave him barely enough time to throw a few necessities into his suitcase before rushing to the airport. *Wait...what? No...he was sitting in the Oval Office with the Speaker and Senate Majority leader earlier that day. Or was that just a dream? Let go, Emery. Let your memories flow.*

Jagged recollections infused into his thoughts like a movie, featuring Emery Clayton as the main character in a set drawn straight from the nineteen sixties. He flashed on an airport counter where he waited for a business associate to arrive. He'd never met either of his travel companions, so he offered only a brief acknowledgement.

When a short, plump man approached, Emery extended a hand.

The man offered a firm shake. "Emery Clayton, I presume. It's nice to put a face to the

5

name. Sorry I'm late. We'd best get going if we're to make our flight."

He checked his watch and nodded. "Damn. You're right."

Both acknowledging they had little time to reach the gate, they dashed through the airport, arriving just as an attendant was closing the flight door. She halted and allowed them to enter. "Must be your lucky day, gentlemen."

Emery stepped aboard and squeezed down the aisle until he found his seat. As he settled in, a wave of nausea grumbled in his stomach, and his head spun. The abrupt departure must have rattled him. *His thoughts jumbled from dreams to reality…but which was which?* Beads of sweat dampened his hairline. Perhaps he needed something to calm his nerves.

He gazed at his companions, then looked away, while new memories flooded the old, shoving his reality into distant corners of his mind. Somehow, he knew these men held high esteem in their fields. Striking a conversation might give him perspective. But what would he say?

"Judging from the weather report, we won't see much during this trip, Mr. Clayton."

Emery had to respond. Talking about the weather seemed benign enough. He turned to face the men sitting across the aisle and searched his disjointed memory…the associate representing Tempest Oil…did he say his name? Emery shot an obvious glance beyond them through a tiny window. "Sure looks that way, Mr.—"

"Hey, don't stand on ceremony. You go by Clay, right?" He didn't wait for an answer. "Just call me Ben. You don't know Lou Rosson, do you?"

Emery couldn't keep up this act for long. Every fiber of his being screamed to understand what was going on. He clenched his jaw and drew in a long breath. *Relax. Just listen and respond.* "Only by reputation." Hand extended, he leaned across the aisle. "Nice to make your acquaintance."

Lou, a lean man with blond, close-cropped hair, craned his neck to see around Ben then smiled, returning the gesture with an outstretched hand that swept past Ben to meet Emery's with a firm grip. "Likewise. We have a long trip ahead so we might as well get comfortable."

As the plane gained altitude, Emery forced himself to relax, tentatively conceding to the new memories now streaming into his thoughts. He let go of his trepidation and allowed the conversation to flow. The three men chatted stopping only when the flight attendant interrupted offering cocktail cards. Having never seen one before, Emery wrinkled his brow and inspected the proffer.

Ben glanced at his watch then studied the drink selections.

"He always checks the time." Lou turned toward Emery. "The greatest loss of time is procrastination. Call it straight, gentlemen, and name your poison."

"Scotch rocks." Emery's reply fell from his lips as if the request was his drink of choice.

"Okay." Ben chuckled. "I'll set aside our schedule and relax. Make that two." He held up two fingers and gave the stewardess a grin.

A soft ding sounded. Emery glanced toward the

cockpit in time to see a no-smoking sign flick off. *Smoking hadn't been allowed on flights since...?* He watched his associates.

Ben leaned into his seat. After tapping a package of Kent cigarettes against his nicotine-stained fingers, he flicked a lighter and lit up then breathed in a long puff before exhaling a white stream through his nose.

Dear Lord, had the entire world slipped into the past? From all indications, yes, yet these men knew him they called him by name. How could that situation be? Tilting his head backward, Emery closed his eyes to feign sleep. Conflicted memories jockeyed for position within his mind. To grasp his situation, he needed to let his thoughts flow and not fight new details. Surely, at some point, he'd understand. As if in a dream, he pondered over the last few days of new memories.

Hectic described the entire week. His boss handed Emery—no, he handed *Clay* this new assignment, and he gave a perfunctory examination of the work involved. *But as President, he had no boss...stop, Emery...for now, forget the presidency...let the new memories flow as if you were injected into the past or reincarnated into someone else's life. Your name is Clay.*

He opened an eye a slit and glanced toward his two companions. They seemed pleasantly congenial, chitchatting now in a line of technological discussion between a geological point of view and engineering aspects. Neither of which interested Emery. He shifted his gaze toward the small window and watched the billowing clouds drift beneath the plane.

The stewardess—not flight attendant—tapped his shoulder to get his attention then handed him a lowball glass and a newspaper. He nodded approval, tucked the paper beside him and sipped the amber liquid. Scotch rocks. This would soothe his jagged nerves.

He glanced at Ben. A faint memory reminded him they spoke over the phone last week. Now, he noted how different the man appeared from the stiff, reserved and rather business-like image Clayton envisioned. Instead, the man was short and plump with a balding spot on top. His brown eyes matched his hair color, and his chubby cheeks had a reddish tinge, as if his collar fit a bit too tight.

Lou, on the other hand, sat tall and lean, obviously in excellent physical condition. Blond close-cropped hair and tanned skin displayed an interest in outdoor sports, and his eyes were blue and steady. The two differed as much as Mutt and Jeff...*Whoever they were.*

Again, Emery sipped a long drink then reached for the newspaper nestled beside him. Unfolding the pages, he glanced at the headline: *Nixon And Kennedy Score Big Victories in New Hampshire.*

Eyes wide, he gulped hard. Was this some kind of a joke? The paper displayed no aging and was dated, March 8, 1960—fifteen years before Emery Clayton was born. If someone crafted this menagerie, the results created one hell of a hoax. He inspected the cabin, noting details impossible to recreate: vintage clothing, no personal devices, an antiquated aircraft, newspapers, smoking on a flight...he scanned the plane searching for just one discrepancy—a Starbucks cup or a cell phone—but he saw nothing tying his surroundings to the twenty-first century. From all indications, President Emery Clayton had literally transported to March 1960.

As president, his briefings included innovative technology and intelligence far beyond the knowledge released to the public. Hell, evidence of the Roswell incident blew him away. He knew prototypes existed connecting past to future but none so precise as what he now experienced. Intentionally relaxing his muscles, he drew in several long breaths. Whatever brought him to this time and place would become clear soon enough.

If China or Russia created this hoax, they had a clear and present motive. But did technology exist to inject new memories into someone's thoughts? Conjuring willpower over emotion, Emery smothered the brigade of ants creeping down his spine. Keeping calm channeled his energy to respond instead of reacting. He had to let the situation unravel. Again, he closed his eyes, this time challenging his resolve to allow invading memories to unfold.

"How about you, Clay?" Lou nudged his arm.

Snapping his gaze to the left, Emery opened his eyes. "I'm sorry. I must have been dosing. What did you say?"

"Ben is such a lady's man. I asked if he ever thought about settling down. I think I'd love having someone to come home to each night. I just haven't found the right woman yet. How about you?"

Emery nodded. "I love my wife and kids. I married the love of my life."

"See. The man agrees with me, Ben."

The two men continued their banter.

He shook his head then tilted it backward against the seat, his thoughts drifting to his wife, Teri...wait, Emery Clayton III was married to Kathleen...and they had two beautiful girls, Madison and Savannah...but...Emery Clayton Senior married a woman named Teri. His pulse raced. Was it possible? Could Emery have been thrust through time to 1960...into his grandfather's life? He wished he had a mirror to verify his theory...maybe he did.

He stood and shuffled down the aisle to the bathroom. Once inside the tiny space, he squeezed his eyes shut and took a deep breath. His heart pounded so hard he heard the thump-thumping despite the whine of the engines. Emery grasped hold of the sink then opened his eyes and stared at his reflection. Holy hell. The mirror image studying Emery was not his own. He could see a familial resemblance, but that man was definitely not Emery Clayton III.

Glaring at the likeness, he twisted his lips...opened his mouth...stuck out his tongue...and contorted his features until the reality set in. Without a doubt, he was gazing at *his* reflection...but the man returning the stare was...Emery Clayton *Senior*...his grandfather. He appeared to be a lot younger than Emery's memory envisioned— but somehow Emery's mind now shared a body with Gramps.

He opened the door and returned to his seat as puzzle pieces began to fall in place. As inexplicable as the premise sounded, somehow, Emery Clayton III no longer existed... at least not yet...not in this era. For the time being...his mind now shared a body with his grandfather.

Squeezing his eyes tightly, he encouraged more memories to flow. Gramps desperately wanted this job. Succeeding would boost his career. No doubt the devil was in the details. The question was, could this Emery Clayton pull off the deal? He knew nothing of his grandfather's work. In fact, to the best of his recollection, Gramps was a US Senator...now that Emery could do with his eyes closed...but accounting? Only time would tell.

What had Emery said or done prior to this shift? He racked his brain to remember how the incident occurred. *Hmm*...he recalled standing next to the Resolute Desk...and running his fingers over an etched insignia carved into the wooden drawer. He'd sat at that desk so many times over the past three years but had never noticed the strange symbol...grabbing his glasses, he squinted to read the inscription. The memory surfaced with a jolt— *"God grant me wisdom to light the way and the strength of our forefathers to save the day."* That's it...

When he read those words aloud, a bluish mist swirled around the room, engulfing him. At first, he gasped for air. But realizing the haze evoked a sense of calm unlike anything he'd ever felt before, he relinquished his mind and body to drift within the cloud...after a moment of elation, he blacked out...when he opened his eyes, his reality had shifted.

Emery had never been a man who believed in

magical occurrences of any sort. But he couldn't deny something beyond his control brought him to this place and time. Perhaps the Resolute Desk held centuries of mystical enchantment...and the incantation he muttered triggered the shift, spiraling him here to find the answers he sought.

If he could believe in time travel devices, the Roswell incident, and more, he had to admit forces existed beyond the realm of common sense. In theory, the powers that be would return him to his own life once he completed their task...unless his hypothesis held no credence. He could think of only one feasible alternative—a heart attack or stroke...was Emery trapped inside his own mind? Was he laying in a hospital...unresponsive...in a coma?

Chapter Two

As President of the United States, Emery struggled for answers, trying desperately to bring together a perilously divided country now peppered with anarchy. Was it possible someone—or something—heard his plea and thrust him into the past to find a solution? Perhaps. Even if he understood precisely what transpired, he still had no way of reversing the incident. The most important lesson he'd learned in life thus far was dwelling on his past—or what he no longer had—paralyzed his present and stole hope for his future.

In his first Inaugural Address, Franklin D. Roosevelt made a profound statement that stuck with Emery ever since he heard the quote. "The only thing we have to fear is fear itself...nameless, unreasoning, unjustified terror, which paralyzes needed efforts to convert retreat into advance." Roosevelt gave the speech to calm panic and hopelessness gripping America during the Great Depression—but the quote inspired Emery so much, he lived by those words. If he let fear take root, his energy drained. Embracing fear was not an option.

For now, he chose to believe he experienced a time slip. Whatever thrust Emery into this place and time, he knew embracing the situation made more sense than struggling to understand. Regardless of whether he lay in a comatose state, was dreaming, or facing an unknown reality, fear would only paralyze his efforts. Until new choices arose, he resolved to live in the moment and react with all the strength and knowledge he could provide. For now, he was Emery Clayton Senior.

Again, he closed his eyes and strained to conjure his grandfather's memories. This time focusing on his wife, Teri. Sinking deeper, now, into his new recollections, he could almost see her pale, tear-streaked face pressed against the window, as she waved a tentative goodbye when he left the house. Gramps knew—no, *Clay* knew his business trips put a lot on her shoulders, especially now that Jenny and Emery, their two children, were older and more energetic.

But this trip caused her more concern than normal. Her reaction to his boss's call had her honestly worried. At first, she acted the part of a cosmopolitan wife, blasé and unpretentious. The tears came later as he rushed to pack. Clay felt helpless when she cried. Thank goodness those occasions were few and far between.

Jenny and Emery added to the strain. They sensed when tension disturbed the normal flow of everyday routine. It's hard to hide emotions from children, even at their ages. They clung to Daddy and burst into tears for the slightest reasons. The last time he left town, they fussed so much he decided to take Teri out for the evening, leaving the children's favorite babysitter to entertain them. Convinced the idea would alleviate the tension, he put his best foot forward, but the entire evening went wrong.

First, Clay forgot his driver's license and was pulled over for going the wrong way down a one-way street, resulting in a ticket. Finally seated for dinner, he inadvertently jostled Teri's arm, spilling her drink down the front of her favorite dress. The restaurant ran out of the item she loved, and the second choice, a strip steak, arrived so well done she barely ate a few bites before pushing the plate aside. By the time they returned home, he knew Teri pretended gaiety neither of them felt.

Clay needed this assignment. He just wished the timing was better. Moving Teri from Augusta, Georgia, her childhood hometown, to the hustle and bustle of Houston, Texas, required a huge adjustment. They transferred less than a month earlier. Barely long enough to unpack, let alone get settled or meet friends. Compared to Houston, Augusta seemed like a one-horse country stop.

The next-door neighbors seemed nice, but they weren't the homefolk Teri loved. Hell, she wasn't much more than a kid herself and Clay left her entirely on her own, in a strange bustling town with two small children. He could only imagine how abandoned she must have felt as he waved goodbye and climbed the stairs to the plane. It was still a major proposition for Teri to take the car into town. She didn't have his built-in radar and though the drive to buy groceries wasn't far, the area was completely unfamiliar.

His life evolved so differently. He left home at seventeen to attend the university and never looked back, returning only for occasional vacations. When he graduated, Smith-Robinson and Company immediately offered him a job. Only twenty-eight and he already felt accomplished. He'd done right well so far, and this job would open doors, allowing him to continue to rise in his accounting profession. Clay learned at an early age to look out for you and yours because nobody else would.

A brief moment of panic surged through him like ice in his veins. Could he really accomplish what was thrown on his plate, pull-off this job and make any sort of show at all. The company bigwigs must have been out of their ever lovin' minds thinking he was ready for this kind of responsibility. If he failed, he'd wind up back in Augusta chewing out figures for other accountants who made the grade. No career, no job security, no salary... no nothing.

He grinned ruefully to himself. Here he was, ready to run home with his tail between his legs before he even got his feet wet. What a bunch of rot he fed Teri about his ideas and ambitions. He was a real hotshot. Clay sat up in his seat and drew his thoughts back to the conversation when Lou asked him a question. "Sorry, what did you say?"

"Just asked how come you got dragged into this assignment, Clay. The job promises to be a long, drawn-out affair with a lot of travel. Not ideal for a family-man like you."

He shrugged. "The bigwigs scheduled Bob Kelsey. He'd run the account for some time, but this trip came up so fast, he couldn't break away from a pending case. I finished my assignment last week, so I guess the logical choice placed me at the helm." Clay grinned, feeling his cheeks heat with the air of uncertainty.

"Come on. If you didn't have the ability, Smith-Robinson wouldn't have accepted you as a replacement. They don't hand out Audit Manager positions to any random pencil-pusher. You've got to be able to cut the mustard."

The comment relaxed Clay's nerves. He drew out his papers and the three settled in, discussing possibilities and probabilities in the New Zealand gas-oil strike. They talked long after the stewardess brought their meals, and by the time the flight circled over Los Angeles, they'd agreed to major decisions regarding the case.

After making their connecting flight to a DC 8 with minimal inconvenience, they boarded and sat in their first-class seats. Clay fastened his seatbelt to prepare for takeoff, leaned back in the seat, and settled in for the flight to Hawaii. The ice broken, he could relax now, knowing the other two men respected his knowledge and proficiency.

To the rear of the plane, in the second-class compartment, James Rucker—listed on the flight manifesto as James X—felt a strong sense of satisfaction. With a good meal under his belt, he drew in a long breath and relaxed his tired muscles. Resting his shoes against the footrest, he pushed back, stretched, and stifled a yawn.

Man, oh man, this is high-class travel. A lot different from hoppin' freights. And he would know about that. He'd hopped his share of trains the last few years. Preparing for the long flight, he leaned into his seat and positioned his head until he found a comfortable spot.

His companion shot him a glance laced with irritation then turned his head and peered out the window.

Anger seething in his gut, James edged closer to the man's seat. "Move over you S-O-B," he whispered in a low, breathy spat. He watched for a response.

The man beside James scowled and angled his shoulder toward the window.

With a chuckle, this time more audible, James snarled. "What? You afraid you'll get some color rubbed off onto you?" He shook his head then settled in for the long trip.

Behind him, a baby wailed. His mother quietly comforted him, rhythmically patting the baby lying against her shoulder. The cry muffled as she hummed a lullaby and rocked him to and fro, whispering into his ear through his tousled blond hair.

The muted hum of the engines must have lulled the baby into sleep as the cries subsided.

The cabin lights dimmed, and the passengers

quieted, most dozing while the plane winged its way through the velvety night sky.

James slept heavily, until the wailing child began crying outright and awakened him. In a groggy fog, he lifted his head and glared over his seatback at the child and mother. Irritated at being aroused so early, he huffed. She should have popped a bottle in the kid's mouth when he started to cry, so as not to bother the other travelers.

When nature called, James shoved his way past the passenger in the adjoining seat and squeezed down the aisle toward the commode. Completely disregarding a man who stood waiting next to the door, he slid in front as another man left, then plowed into the room, and slammed the door before the waiting man could respond. Once inside the tiny room he flushed the sleep from his eyes. Anger seething from a lifetime of disrespect, James took his time. When he heard the telecom announce the flight's imminent arrival, he slowly sauntered out of the restroom, ignoring blatant stares and disgusted expressions thrown his way as he returned to his seat.

Thankful the baby in the tail section was quiet, James sat and refastened his seatbelt, anxious for the trip to be over.

Chapter Three

A single tear escaped and trickled onto Teri's cheek. Biting her lower lip, she wiped away the moisture with the back of her hand then scanned the parking lot to get her bearings. The sun that sat low on the horizon when she and Clay arrived at the airport now hid behind threatening clouds. Driving home in the dark on unfamiliar roads would be challenging, but add a storm to the mix? She'd best get on the road right away.

After studying the directions Clay wrote earlier that morning, she slipped the car into gear and flashed a glance over her shoulder before backing out of the parking slot. Taking a right onto the ramp, she increased her speed to that of the surrounding traffic. The straight shot to and from the airport seemed simple enough, but the route required her to navigate the confusing Houston Interstate loops.

Tiny splashes of rain dotted the windshield. She flipped on the wipers then tightened her grip on

23

the steering wheel and focused on the road ahead. Distracted by the cars whishing past, she almost missed her exit. She jerked the wheel to the left and, in a blare of honking horns, glanced in the rearview mirror. A jolt of adrenaline shot down her neck and clenched her stomach. Realizing how close she'd come to crashing into the car in the next lane, she breathed in a gasp of relief.

Rain peppered the windshield with angry drops. Exiting the ramp, she turned left, thankful to be off the Interstate and in semi-familiar territory, but the incident left her shaken. Teri drew in a deep breath and relaxed her grip on the steering wheel then turned on the radio. After listening to the tail end of a news report, she dialed the tuner to find some music and caught a station playing *Sentimental Journey*, one of her favorite songs. Humming to the tune, her thoughts turned to Clay.

Clay hesitated to show his excitement despite the opportunities the job offered, for fear she would become upset. Once again, she proved him right. Why did she freeze at the thought of him flying so far away? He certainly couldn't walk to Australia.

Breathing in deeply, Teri calmed her nerves, rationalizing her unfounded fears. Everything would be all right. He'd be perfectly safe. How many times had Clay explained the dynamics of flying? Flying is safer than driving in a car.

Again, tears sprung to her eyes and she swallowed hard to dissipate them. "Take care of yourself, Clay. We'd be so lost without you," she whispered into the night.

Cognitively, she knew her fear of flying was

irrational, but she couldn't shake the feeling of impending doom that threatened to engulf her when she thought of this trip. Clay flew innumerable times before and she had worried, but she'd managed to temper the jittery sensation. Why not this time? Perhaps because everything piled on her at once, like moving to Houston, changing the children's schools, and not knowing anyone, or the lay of the land.

The car hydroplaned, returning her thoughts to the moment. The rain pelted the car in violent sheets. Thank God she was almost home. She pulled into the driveway as close to the front door as possible, parked, then opened the door latch and sprinted into the house. The front room lamp lit her way through to the rec room where the babysitter read a story to the children. The girl stopped as Teri entered, put the book on the top of coffee table, and sprung to her feet.

"I hope the children have behaved well, Janet. How much do I owe you?"

"It hasn't been quite two hours, Mrs. Clayton. Is $0.75 okay? The children have been really good."

"Here's a dollar, honey. You don't know how much we appreciate you coming." Teri glanced outside. "It's raining pretty hard, now. Do you want me to drive you home?"

"No, ma'am. Please don't bother. I've got my raincoat. It will just take a second to run down the street."

After Janet slipped into her coat, Teri walked outside, stood on the porch. Lightning struck like a sheet across the sky with jagged bolts horizontally then downward. Teri jumped at the crack and trembled, almost forgetting her task. She searched the street just in time to see Janet rush across her front yard and into the house. Brushing the mist from her sleeves, she gazed up and down the street then went inside and shut the door behind her. Again, a violent crash of thunder boomed, sending a shiver down her back. Slipping off her own damp jacket, she snatched a hanger from the hall closet then hung her wrap on the rack, pushing the others aside so hers would dry.

Emery and Jenny begged her to finish the story Janet was reading, so Teri sat on the couch and pulled them close, happy to have the diversion. "And so little two-shoes married the handsome prince and lived happily ever after." Laying the book on the coffee table, Teri glanced at the clock. The children had school the next day ,and she wanted to stick to their bedtime schedule. "Just about time to eat, kids. I think your favorite show is on. You two watch television while I prepare your dinner." She tuned the TV to *Leave it to Beaver* then strolled toward the kitchen to fix supper.

The house felt damp and chilly. She rubbed her hands over her arms, flipped on the light then turned the oven to preheat. She pulled some minute-steaks from the fridge and popped them inside to bake. The steak sent a delicious aroma swirling through the air and the oven heat warmed the room. She opened a can of green beans, dumped them in a pot then whipped up a batch of quick potatoes.

Placing the children's plates in front of them,

she finally took her seat and blessed the food. Emery dawdled over his meal as usual, but once he finished, she got the two children tubbed, scrubbed, and ready for bed. After listening to their prayers, she tucked them in and kissed them good night.

When she returned to the kitchen, she washed the supper dishes, then picked up a magazine and trudged upstairs with every intention of reading in bed. She showered then slipped into her nightgown. Nine-thirty p.m. already. The day wore her down and she couldn't wait to slip under clean sheets and snuggle into cozy blankets. Snatching her magazine, she settled into bed and thumbed through the pages.

In the distance, thunder rolled a soothing tone, but when a crack hit close by, she sat up with a jolt. Shaking her head at her nervousness, she laid aside the magazine. A plane flying overhead caught her attention, and she shivered, hoping Clay's flight wouldn't hit stormy weather. The thought triggered a wave of cold heat to clench the back of her neck.

As she leaned forward to glance outside, she caught a glimpse of Clay's picture on her side table. Drawing it close, she ran a finger over his image. His strong features, deep brown hair, and crystal blue eyes melted her heart the moment they'd met, and despite the years, her pulse still raced at the thought of his embrace. A soft smile tugged at the corners of her mouth as she stared at the picture. His eyes still twinkled, and his smile calmed her. "Good night, darling," she whispered sleepily. She kissed two fingers then pressed them against the glass before returning the picture to its spot on the side table. When the clock chimed 10:00 p.m., she flipped off the light then closed her eyes and drifted into slumber.

The next morning, Teri readied the children for nursery school. After walking them to their classes, she returned home and straightened the house. At 10 o'clock, the phone rang. Though she expected the call, she picked up with a sinking sensation coiling in her stomach.

"Western Union ma'am. We have a telegram for Mrs. E. J. Clayton."

After holding her breath for a brief moment, she spoke. "This is she."

"The message is as follows:

'Darling, arrived in Hawaii as scheduled—stop. Rosson and Moore are very pleasant—stop. Weather okay, flight good—stop. Should arrive on schedule—stop. Will cable from Australia—stop. Expect a package from me—stop.

Love Clay…

"Would you like a copy of the cable, ma'am?"

"Yes, please." Teri hung up the phone and let out a relieved breath. The sun shone brightly outside, and she hummed a tune as she finished cleaning. By 10:30, she was dressed and ready to go to the store. After putting on her coat and scarf, she glanced in the mirror, checked her lipstick, picked up her purse, and rushed out the door for a frivolous day of shopping.

Chapter Four

L ou stirred when the stewardess brushed against his seat as she scurried down the aisle. Opening his eyes, he watched her busily prepare for early risers. *A perky gal... Bobbie something-or-other...Russell, that was it, Bobbie Russell.* His sleepy thoughts wandered. When she whisked by again, his gaze met hers. He offered a drowsy nod then whispered, "Hey honey, can you bring me a cup of coffee?"

She smiled and put her finger to her lips. Moments later, it seemed to Lou, she stood next to him, this time offering a steamy cup and holding another for herself.

Taking her proffer, he drew the brew close to his lips and inhaled the aroma as he sipped. *To his mind, this was a perfect cup of coffee. As black as the ace of spades and as welcome as a weekend paycheck.* Grinning, he motioned her to sit.

She hesitated a moment before slipping into the empty seat beside him.

His heart beat wildly when her hair brushed over his shoulder as she settled into the seat.

"So, Mr. Rosson, are you headed home or visiting Hawaii to relax in paradise?"

Delighted she showed interest in him, he wondered what caught her attention. He never thought of himself as much of a lady's man. Perhaps his eyes. People had often mentioned his ice-blue eyes were striking. "Neither, I'm afraid. I'll only be in Honolulu long enough to catch a connecting flight."

"That's too bad. The island is beautiful."

Lou recognized a southern drawl but ask anyway. "Where you from, honey child?"

Her eyelashes fluttered. She couldn't deny her southern roots. Wrapping her hands around the warm cup, she drew it to her lips and gazed at Lou while she sipped, then put her cup down and spoke. "Why Mistuh Rosson, I declare, yoah approach is so original. I actually hail from Atlanta, and ah'm right proud of that." She tittered. "I thought I'd lost most of my accent, but you're correct. I was born and raised in Atlanta, Georgia."

Lou chuckled and crinkled his eyes. "Darlin' you could cut your drawl with a knife and spread it on bread with honey."

She smiled, clearly accepting his comment as a compliment as opposed to a tease.

Lou immediately felt an attraction. A woman who could banter with him without hesitation brought a smile to his lips. He studied her face…a cute turned-up nose, dancing brown eyes, and light brown hair with golden flecks that caught the early dawn light beaming through the window. A warm tingle buzzed between his hips, causing him to adjust his position. Glancing out the window, he paused to watch the first rays of sun break through the clouds, casting a panorama of an almost spiritual quality against the wing. Without facing her, he felt for her hand and slipped it into his as if he'd known her for years.

The action didn't faze her. Whispering softly to avoid disturbing the other passengers, they chatted intimately, and in those few moments they learned more about each other than many knew after years of dating.

Rustling in his seat, Clay opened his eyes and peeked across the aisle toward Lou and Bobbie then closed them again and lay there quietly for a few more minutes before he yawned and stretched his arms.

Lou sat straight and leaned forward. Assuming Clay feigned sleep so as not to intrude, he cleared his throat and whispered. "Care to join us for a hot cup of brew?"

Again, Clay yawned then apologized to no one in particular. Stretching his neck side to side, he gazed at Lou. "A cup of coffee is definitely in order."

Immediately, Bobbie stood and slipped into the aisle.

Lou excused himself and scuffed toward the lavatory then squeezed inside the tiny room. After relieving himself, he washed his hands then pushed open the door, forcing Clay to take a step backward. Lou chuckled. "Sorry." He squeezed by him and switched positions.

"Fresh coffee awaits you back at your seat." Clay announced over his shoulder then eased into the lavatory compartment.

Lou strolled back to his chair, meeting Bobbie with fresh coffee in hand on his way. He smiled and took the cup. "Just what I needed," he whispered, squeezing past her. "Come sit a while longer." He glanced around. "No one else is awake yet."

She nodded. "All right, but just for a few more minutes. Everyone will be waking soon and requesting breakfast."

When Clay returned, Lou nudged him. "Bobbie hails from your neck of the woods." He snapped his fingers. "Oh blast, forever forgetting the niceties." He turned to her. "Bobbie, this is Mr. Emery Clayton." His gaze glued to hers, he concluded the introduction. "Clay, meet Miss Roberta Russell. She's from Atlanta."

"I'm right pleased to make your acquaintance, Mistuh Clayton."

Hearing her thick drawl again, Lou smiled.

She raised a brow, peering at Lou from the corner of her eye then turned toward Clay. "So nice to meet a Southern gentleman."

Clay caught her surreptitious glance and smiled. "It's just Clay, ma'am."

Voices low, the three chatted until the rest of the passengers showed signs of stirring.

Having finished her second cup, Bobbie stood and excused herself to attend to her duties.

Ben, awakening from a sound sleep, turned his head and cocked an eye at his companions. "What?

Everyone was invited to this soirée but me?" He straightened his slumped position. "Where's my coffee?"

"Ah, the wench must be neglecting her duties." Lou grumbled, making sure Bobbie could hear his exaggerated complaint.

Bobbie grinned then turned toward the galley. From then on, until the Captain announced their approach to the mainland, she stayed busy.

Settling into his seat, Lou idly watched her dash back and forth as passengers demanded her attention with a need for everything from aspirin to safety pins. Finally turning toward Ben, he waited until he felt sure she was within hearing distance then fired a comment. "I guess the more pleasing possibilities of connubial bliss have escaped me...until now."

Bobbie's cheeks flushed. She wrinkled her forehead and her eyes widened briefly before she turned her attention to another passenger.

Clay faced Ben and changed the subject to the geological estimates of reserves they received from the New Zealand firm.

In no way would Lou allow shop talk to divert his attention. Continuing to eye Bobbie, his heart beat wildly each time she brushed by. Her extenuated wiggle teased him as she pranced up and down the aisle, attending to passengers. Something about this woman shot tingles in all the right places. It wasn't pure lust, though he definitely desired her. Was it her quirky quips or the sensual way she fluttered her lashes? He didn't know, but he couldn't take his eyes off Bobbie—until she disappeared into the galley. Only then did he return his attention to his cohorts.

Ben, now fortified with caffeine, glanced toward Clay. "It's a good thing we change stewardesses in Hawaii," —he hitched his chin toward Lou—"or we wouldn't get a lick of work from this guy."

Lou forced an injured look. "This one has no room to talk. I've seen him operate before, and there's no stopping him once he sets his sight on a gal." Again, Lou's glance shot toward Bobbie. "So, help me Hannah, I believe this woman just might be the real thing. That little gal is what I've been searching for all my life."

Ben raised a brow. "I've always seen you as a perpetual bachelor."

Lou dropped his gaze and lowered his voice. "Believe me, Ben. This girl has my heart doing flip-flops. She's really different from those other gals."

Ben pinched his brows together. "Temptation rarely comes during work hours. The trouble with you is... you don't work enough." He shook his head then turned toward Clay. "About those estimates...Lou mentioned on the way to the gate this morning that he'd have to study the electric logs and other such data before determining the reliability of the numbers..."

With a tray of coffee balanced on the palm of her hand, Bobbie swished past Lou. She gazed over her shoulder. "The flight crew calls." She smiled, then whooshed down the aisle and disappeared into the cockpit.

Reluctantly, Lou gave up his visual pursuit and

joined Ben and Clay's discussion.

When the men's room sign switched to unoccupied, Ben downed his coffee, then stood. Headed toward the door, he glanced over his shoulder. "Shelf the discussion, gentlemen. I'll return directly."

Lou shifted his gaze toward Clay. "We'll be landing shortly. No sense getting embroiled in business at this point, anyway."

Clay nodded then turned toward the window. "Looks like a storm is brewing. We might have a turbulent flight tonight."

Lou peered past Clay toward the darkening clouds threatening the small aircraft, his thoughts still swirling around Bobbie. "I wonder what genius said a man should work as if he'll live forever but live as if he'll die today?" He grinned. "Whomever said that is my kind of guy."

Chapter Five

T he morning sunlight gleamed through the tiny window as beams reflected off the wing of the DC-8. Prying his eyelids open, Clay peered outside then squinted. The previous evening's stormy weather had dissolved into the night sky and now the morning sparkled with gold and crimson splashing across azure blue.

Moments before the jet's landing gear lowered, a voice boomed over the speaker, "Ladies and gentlemen, we are approaching our final destination and will be landing in beautiful Honolulu, Hawaii shortly. Please fasten your seatbelts and stay seated until the plane comes to a complete stop."

Taking the later flight allowed Clay and the other businessmen to arrive in Honolulu early enough to avoid crowds and typical airport confusion. The later Hawaiian flights would be met with a stream of smiling Polynesians offering leis to travelers as they disembarked.

When the door opened, a ground attendant

pushed a rolling ramp into place. Clay gazed through his cabin window and noted the passengers entering the building without the nuisance of vendors pandering their wares. When most of the tourists had disappeared into the airport, Clay, Lou, and Ben prepared to deplane.

"Don't know about you two, but I'm hungry enough to eat a horse." Lou ducked his head and entered the aisle to join his cohorts. Once they found their way through the terminal, the three men headed for the first restaurant they could find that served breakfast.

A bar and grill with a flickering neon sign flashed above and to their right. When Clay opened the door, tantalizing aromas encircled him, enticing his growling stomach with sizzling bacon mingled with fresh coffee and fried eggs. He strolled inside and slipped into the first available booth.

Once seated, they all snatched their menus and studied the offerings, while a woman swiped the table with a damp cloth then set utensils on napkins. A busboy balancing a tray of glasses filled to the brim with iced water appeared and set one before each of them.

Dressed in a white uniform with a folded red handkerchief flowered on her shoulder, the waitress tugged at her red-trimmed apron then pulled a pencil from behind her ear and stood ready to take orders. "What can I bring you this fine morning, gentlemen?"

Clay spoke first. "I'll have a plate of bacon and eggs, sunny side up, please."

"Coffee, sir?"

"Yes, please. Cream and sugar. Thank you."

She turned toward Ben. "And for you, sir?"

"Make that two."

Lou glanced at the waitress's nametag and flashed a toothy grin. "Peggy, honey, anything you bring couldn't help but be wonderful."

She shot him a gaze, her face softening from a fixed smile to an honest grin. "Mister, for you I'll bring the best in the house. How's about pomelo in sherry and passion fruit, a rasher of bacon broiled in pineapple juice, scrambled eggs, buttered toast with guava jelly, and coffee, hot and steamin'?"

Nodding, Lou approved her suggestion with a big smile.

Peggy hurried off toward the kitchen with their order in hand.

Ben snorted. "Passion fruit? That's the one thing you don't need." He chuckled.

Lou studied the two men for a moment. "You two old married folks have lost all your passion. You've settled into complacency to the point where you eat solely to satisfy hunger pains. Thanks... but no, thank you. Half the pleasure of eating is to savor the wonderful different tastes. I'll take the passion fruit every time."

Ben turned toward Clay and hitched his head in Lou's direction, "This guy eats, loves, and lives extravagantly."

"I beg to differ. I'm not extravagant. I simply choose to live life to the fullest...I enjoy every day as if it was my last and try to give each person I meet a reason to smile."

Clay observed his companions in amusement.

39

The two men were easily ten to fifteen years his senior, but he had a feeling working with them would never be dull. In doing so, he was sure the experience would be a constant soirée.

On the job though, he had no doubt these two men functioned with razor-sharp minds. What a bunch of characters. He shook his head in silence.

Lou faced Clay in time to see his gesture. "Ben, I do believe this lad has given up hope on us."

Clay readied himself for an expected verbal bombardment. When the front door opened, he snapped a gaze toward the sound.

"Saved by the bell." Ben cocked his head toward Bobbie as she pranced through the entrance accompanied by a tall redheaded stewardess roughly thirty years old.

In a gallant gesture, Lou shot to his feet. He winked at Bobbie then swept a hand toward the booth in an exaggerated bow. "Ladies, please join us poor working men in a bit of a repast."

Again, Clay shook his head, unsure whether Lou exemplified the world's biggest philanderer or if the man had actually been swept off balance by the pretty stewardess and an unforgettable connection.

The redhead gazed at Lou with a cold stare. "I abhor that word... poor." She turned toward Bobbie. "Are these strange creatures actually friends of yours?"

Face flushed, Bobbie shot him a wink. "It seems to me the dimwitted one who bowed at our approach looks vaguely familiar, Chris. From what I've seen so far, he's quite harmless."

"Well then, shall we join them? I always

appreciate a meal more if I'm not on the receiving end of the check." Chris chortled.

As the men scooted closer to make room for the two women, Bobbie introduced Chris and the group chitchatted until Peggy approached to take the ladies' orders.

In a small booth behind them, James Rucker sat listening to their boisterous conversation. Though he arrived well before the three men, his order had yet to be taken. He scowled then whistled to grab the waitress's attention and motioned with a firm gesture, demanding service.

Nonchalantly gazing in his direction and clearly annoyed at his rudeness, Peggy rolled her eyes and waved him off then took orders from patrons at another table.

When she turned toward the kitchen, again, James whistled. This time loud enough to turn several heads.

With a shrug, she strolled toward him, order book in hand, but stopped three feet from his table. "What'll it be?"

James half hoped she'd refuse to serve him service so he could raise a commotion, but she waited to take his order. "I'll have two fried eggs over easy, sausage, and toast."

"Coffee?"

"Yes. Black."

"As the ace of spades," she muttered then

strolled toward the kitchen.

His glare shot daggers in her wake. Her blatant revulsion irked his soul. How dare that waitress ignore him then offer a such a blasé attitude, as if taking his order caused her inconvenience. Treating him differently than all the white folks…as if being black made him some dumb, subhuman annoyance. The arrogance infuriated James. Those uppity whites and their silent disapproval set his teeth on edge. He'd like to cram their righteous indignation down their gullets… and maybe he would before he was through with this plan.

When the waitress returned with his meal, she set the plate on the side of the table then spun and marched toward the kitchen.

After one bite, he called across the dining room. "Hey, waitress. These fried eggs are too well done and lukewarm at best. Bring me another plate and this time make sure the eggs are hot." He pushed the plate to the middle of the table.

The waitress stopped cold, glared over her shoulder and frowned. Turning, she sauntered to his table, snatched up his dish in stony silence then meandered through the swinging doors into the kitchen. Minutes later, she brought out a hot plate and set the food before him.

He took a bite and nodded. "Do you know what over easy means?" He shook his head. "At least the eggs are warm this time." Dismissing the waitress, he turned his thoughts to the job ahead. *A day will come when those holier-than-thou whites will rue the day they enslaved my ancestors and demeaned my people.*

Chapter Six

Seat angled so he saw the entire restaurant affair play out, Lou watched the colored man eat his breakfast, following each clenched forkful with a drink of coffee. Anger seething, he pinched his facial features into a tight scowl. After cleaning his plate, he marched to the cashier and paid his bill, bitterly complaining at the poor service he received.

When the waitress returned to Lou's table to refill coffee cups, he smiled. Hitching his chin after the patron, Lou wrinkled his forehead. "What the devil brought on that display?"

She shook her head. "Sometimes folks come in here looking for trouble, and if they don't find it, they create a scene."

"I sure hope that second plateful won't come out of your salary."

"It would have." She leaned closer and smirked. "I simply slipped the eggs onto a hot plate. I figured he'd never know the difference." She straightened her back. "Looks like I was right."

Bobbie wiped her lips with a napkin then placed the linen beside her empty plate. "That guy seemed like he wanted to cause a ruckus." Her gaze drifted to Lou. "He acted so angry on the plane, I checked the flight manifest to see who he was. He listed his name as James X…like Malcom X, you know? The man who says the demise of the devil white race is imminent. I hope this man isn't violent."

Lou patted her hand. "I wouldn't be too worried about that." He gazed at the doorway where the black man exited. "Who knows what he's gone through, Bobbie. We all have our crosses to bear…his must feel awful heavy lately."

Lou peered at the bill on the table and slid his hand over it then drew it close.

"I'll take care of that." Clay held out a hand toward Lou.

"Why don't we go Dutch?" Ben asked.

Lou chuckled and dug his wallet from his pocket then stood. "This bill won't break the bank. I've got it." He strolled toward the cashier.

Sifting through her purse, Bobbie followed him.

Lou held a splayed hand toward her. "Honey, I'm mighty pleased you can't bear to be away from me, but I think my expense account can manage this bill. All right?" He bantered in an easy tone but was dead serious about paying her bill. A gentleman never lets a woman pay for a meal. After picking up a newspaper and some mints, he paid the cashier.

The rest of the group caught up with Lou and

Bobbie as they left the breakfast shop and strolled outside, again chitchatting. The two ladies strode alongside the men as they made their way toward the ticket counter to check their flight connections.

With the second leg of the businessmen's flight complete, they still had one more plane to catch to their final destination. Finding they had seven more hours of layover before takeoff, the group stood to one side of the desk and discussed what they would do to fill the afternoon.

Acknowledging Bobbie and Chris had free time as well, Lou immediately took each by the arm, leaving the two married men to call their wives and search for souvenirs to send home as gifts. Lou glanced over his shoulder and shot them a cheerful smile.

Clay and Ben shook their heads and chuckled as Lou strolled away with a woman hooked on each arm.

After a few minutes of walking, Chris met a friend and left Lou and Bobbie to wander the shops together.

He relished the time alone with her. From morning through afternoon was a blur of excitement, as they visited dozens of tourist shops. Each filled to the brim with handmade trinkets and bright-colored apparel. Eager shopkeepers and cordial Polynesians sold leis made from hibiscus, ginger, and ylang-ylang, all vying for attention as they displayed their wares.

Lou bought two gardenia and orchid leis and slipped one over Bobbie's head then draped the other around his neck. The soft scent of the mingling flowers relaxed the tension in his back and shoulders that had cramped over the course of the long flight.

"I have an idea." She stopped at a phone booth and made a call. When she hung up, she turned to Lou. "You're going to love me for this."

He grinned. "I don't think that's much of a jump." He stared at her, hoping the connection would last longer than a one-night stand. As much as he teased the other fellas about being tied to a ball and chain, he longed to find a lasting relationship. He'd spent a lifetime looking for a woman who would keep him off balance and captivated. He'd all but given up believing that one woman would sweep into his life—until now. Bobbie made his pulse race from the moment he saw her, and he prayed they could hold on to whatever was between them when they got back to their real lives. So, love? Yes. He could easily fall in love with this woman.

She lowered her chin and blushed then raised her gaze to meet his. "Seriously, Lou. I have a friend who lives a few minutes from here. She says we can borrow her jeep...you sir, are about to embark on my personal grand tour of the island. Then I'm taking you into Honolulu, to Diamondhead, and Waikiki Beach." Her smile beamed ear to ear.

"What a gal."

A few minutes later, they were on the road. By the time they stopped for lunch, both were exhausted. Absorbed in each other, they cared little about what food they ordered. Instead, they sat and nibbled on hors d'oeuvres, drank pina coladas, and laughed together for over an hour.

After eating far more than he planned, Lou took her hand and strolled down the beach, fingers interlaced with hers. Deciding to spend the rest of his time with Bobbie in a more intimate setting, he guided her to a secluded spot on a narrow white coral beach and sat under a grove of palm trees. Kicking off his shoes, he savored the summer sun as it warmed his bare skin. A soft breeze gently blew, swaying through the palms and kissing the tiny white caps as they tossed to-and-fro across the surface.

Sunbeams reflected off Bobbie's light brown hair, highlighting golden strands that glistened as they danced on the breeze. She leaned on her elbows and crossed her feet, her toes stretching toward the blue-green surf. "This beach is a tiny slice of heaven." She turned, propped her back against Lou's chest and dug her bare feet into the sand.

When she tilted her head upward to face the sun, Lou breathed in the soft scent of her hair. He gazed down the length of her body, the sensual lines of her figure holding him spellbound.

Sitting in silence, he watched a lone surfer riding waves in the distance, expertly catching breakers at the precise moment to perch on top and glide to the shore. In the distance, Diamondhead pierced the sky opposite the Paul Tower, soaring hundreds of feet through the afternoon haze.

A soft wind blew a wisp of hair into Bobbie's face and Lou gently tucked the loose strand behind her ear.

She smiled.

He crooked a finger and gently ran it over her forehead to her nose. When he reached her mouth, she pursed her lips, and he pressed a finger against the soft, pink skin. Drawing her close, he kissed her gently. "Has anyone told you how breathtaking you are?"

She shrugged.

"You deserved to be told often. I'll make that my business to remind you."

Bobbie turned and stretched her arms around the back of his head then drew him closer into a long, hot kiss. When their lips parted, he took her hand in his and kissed her fingertips. They coiled together against the soft sand in a passionate embrace, cooled only by the whisper of the soft breeze.

After Lou disappeared around a corner with Bobbie and Chris, Clay and Ben headed toward the telegraph office. They sent wires to their wives acknowledging their safe arrival in Hawaii then both men strolled through the souvenir shops and concessions to see what the stores had to offer. The market brimmed with endless trinkets. Clay mused how they'd stumbled upon a Polynesian Mardi Gras. Racks filled with muumuus and grass skirts, brightly flowered shirts, and sarongs lined tables loaded with monkey pod trays, wooden salad sets, carved figurines, Hawaiian candies, and toys.

Clay found a Polynesian muumuu for Jenny and a toy surfer for Emery, while Ben picked out a beautifully carved figurine that caught his eye. Wanting something a little more personal for Teri, Clay sifted through endless trays of jewelry until he found a pair of blue-tinted oriental earrings, with a pagoda design carved into the stone. He knew the moment he saw them Teri would love the set. She adored jewelry, especially delicate pieces with etched designs, and blue was her favorite color. Disregarding the exorbitant cost, he purchased them, then slipped the gift into his pocket. When he and Ben left the shop, they found a postal store where they could wrap the treasures and mail them home. With plenty of time to spare, they wandered through the concessions until lunchtime.

Returning to the restaurant where they ate breakfast, they ordered a light lunch. The café had calmed considerably after the breakfast rush, so the two lingered over their meal and discussed the New Zealand project. After they ate, they strolled the area, stopping by an overlook to watch jets take off and land. Clay thought how excited Emery would be to see the planes fly right over his head so close he felt as if he could almost touch them. And Teri…she'd love the beaches, palm trees, and shops. What fun she and Jenny would have wandering through the shops and sunning themselves on these snow-white beaches. He resolved to return to Hawaii with his family someday.

Shortly before the plane boarded, Clay and Ben strolled into the airport lounge and sat by the windows in some man-sized leather chairs. He picked up a magazine and leafed through the pages, not noticing Lou and Bobbie arrived until he heard Lou's voice.

Donning a loud orange and red Hawaiian shirt and an armful overloaded with packages, Lou hitched his chin toward Clay.

"You come bearing gifts." Clay chuckled.

Ben shot them a glance. "How did you ever manage to pick up so much junk, Lou? Looks like you both need a keeper."

Lou ignored the remark, dumped the packages onto a nearby couch then straightened his lei. "What a wonderful vacation spot. The people here are terrific, Ben. You should have come along."

Clay gave the two a searching glance. "I think we would have cramped your style, buddy."

Bobbie blushed, her cheeks a brilliant red.

"You'll have to book an entire jet to get those packages home." Ben stood and pulled up two more chairs. "Here, sit and take a load off."

"Bobbie's connections on the mainland found us a jeep, and we took a grand tour of the island, including Honolulu, Diamondhead, Waikiki Beach, and wait until you see what I bought."

Ben shook his head. "From the looks of that load, you must have closed out the shops."

Lou and Bobbie sat and began opening packages.

"This one's for Jenny, Clay." Lou opened a small box and tossed the package. "I hope your daughter will like it."

The box held a small doll with long black hair,

wearing a light blue floral muumuu. A hula skirt nestled beside her. The doll replicated native Polynesians. "Lou, this is so kind of you. I'm sure Jenny will love this little doll. But you really shouldn't have—"

"Not another word. We had fun searching for these little trinkets. Our afternoon couldn't have been any more perfect." He gazed toward Bobbie. "Right, beautiful?"

She grinned. "He's right, Clay. We enjoyed finding souvenirs for everyone."

"Thank you, Lou."

"You're welcome." He shifted his gaze. "Here, Ben, something we thought you'd appreciate." Lou tossed him a small bag.

Digging into the sack, he drew out a gold tie clip with a hula girl stretched out on what appeared to be a sandy beach. "You shouldn't have, Lou."

Lou chuckled. "We couldn't resist." Turning, he lobbed another box to Clay. "This one is for Emery."

He opened the box and smiled. "A toy airplane with Hawaii scripted on the side. What a perfect gift. Emery loves airplanes. Thank you."

"Happy the little guy will get a kick out of my gift." Spying a small box, Lou handed it to Bobbie.

"Oh, Lou, you said this was for your girl." Bobbie's smile faded. "Do you want me to take it stateside and send it?"

He shook his head. "This gift has already reached its destination, Bobbie." He unwrapped the package to reveal a beautifully etched locket. Withdrawing the piece from the tissue paper, he slipped the necklace around her neck, then carefully fastened the catch.

Her smile beamed. "I'll cherish this," she whispered. "And keep it close to my heart until we're together again."

"I'll hold you to that." Lou winked then turned to Clay. "Here's something we thought your wife might like, Clay." He grabbed another present and chucked the box.

Clay caught the present and was about to thank Lou again but noticed how enthralled he was with Bobbie and decided he'd wait until a better time. He stared at the couple. Lou was absolutely smitten.

Bobbie's gaze clung to the necklace. "It's so lovely, Lou," she whispered.

His face flushed with a proud grin. He squeezed her wrist. They stood then strode hand-in-hand toward the door. As they stepped outside, Lou called over his shoulder toward Ben and Clay, "Hey, you two, it's about time to check in. Bobbie and I will see if the flight plans to leave on time." He wrapped an arm around her shoulder and nuzzled her neck as he whispered in her ear. "We'll be back shortly." The door closed gently behind them.

Clay turned toward Ben, barely noticing the black figure eyeballing them from across the room.

Chapter Seven

A smug look on his face, James Rucker sat on the lounge platform where he could see most of the traffic buzzing through the terminal. The newspaper on his lap, which he had yet to read, slid to the floor. Stiff and tired, having not slept well on the previous leg of his trip, he roiled about the snub he was given at breakfast and his anger seethed further with an unexpected flight delay.

Listening-in to the conversation below, James stood and edged toward the door. He'd eavesdropped on the group since the moment he noticed the man and woman walk through the airport lounge with an armful of souvenirs. Remembering the duo from the breakfast grill, he knew they witnessed his skirmish with the waitress. The last thing he wanted was to be judged by a cracker. He wanted to look them in the eye…let them know he was a force to be reckoned with.

When he saw the dapper fella approaching the

exit, James stood. With precise timing, he reached the door at exactly the same moment as the man and shoved forward, ramming whitey as he entered.

James's glare met the man's, icy and stiff.

"Sorry, son." He side-stepped to the right. "The sun is so bright outside I couldn't see you approaching." He turned toward his friends and walked away.

James tightened his face and clenched his fists. Was that man trying to insult his intelligence or was his dark inside comment a direct slur about the color of Jim's skin?

One of the man's friends jumped up and rushed forward. "Hey Lou, is our flight boarding yet?"

James fumed at the murmurs he heard as the men returned to their seats. Did they think his black skin made him deaf, too?

"Damn." Lou said. "The guy caught me off guard."

"You don't think he ran into you on purpose, do you?" Clay asked.

Ben pinched his brows together. "Based on what I saw, damn right. I sure do. Those colored folks act like the world owes them a living."

Again, James clenched his fists and edged closer to the edge of the platform above them, still eavesdropping as they whispered.

"That guy has a chip on his shoulder the size of a boulder and he's set on kicking the whole cotton-pickin' world in the teeth." Ben added.

Lou shook his head. "I wonder what happened to him…personally, I mean, to have developed such rage."

James scowled. The world happened, that's what. Damn those crackers. Just like all whites...but they were right about one thing. James wanted a confrontation. The rage seething inside needed a release to diffuse the imminent combustion. Mumbling under his breath, he stared, filled with the pure, unadulterated loathing of twenty-eight years.

Shooting a glance at James, Lou wrinkled his brow.

But Jim wasn't about to be intimidated.

Lou hitched his chin toward the exit, speaking loudly enough for James to hear. "The plane arrived a few minutes ago, and we'll be boarding in short order. We best get a move on or we'll miss our flight."

Was the idiot goading Jim...or informing him they were leaving and would soon be out of his life?

The group strolled outside, followed by other passengers, until James sat in the lounge alone, plotting his next move. With heated anticipation, he stood and slammed through the door then rushed toward the gate.

With one eye on his companions, Lou stood to one side with Bobbie, whispering sweet nothings into her ear, while Clay waited with Ben. They allowed all the other passengers to board before Clay finally called out. "The pilot is going to leave us behind if we don't get on the plane soon, Lou."

Lou gazed up briefly and nodded. "You two go ahead. I'll meet you there in a jiffy." He returned to his conversation. Digging into his pockets for a pencil, he found a stub then grabbed his pocket secretary.

"Address, young lady? We ought, with any luck, to know how long this job will take within a couple of weeks. I want to write you. When I arrive in L.A. on my way home...I'd love to get together again...if it's alright with you."

"Sounds interesting, sir." She offered a coy grin. "I know of several places you would enjoy. I live in an apartment uptown with my roommate. Los Jacarandas, Apartment C, 10.

Lou scribbled the address into his notebook.

Peeking over the tablet, she sighed. "Just how many addresses do you have in your little black book?"

He shot her a quick gaze and returned the writing utensils to his pocket then, catching a hold of her waist, he pulled her close. After tilting her chin upward until her gaze met his, he kissed her soft, pink lips... long and hard. "You don't have to worry about anyone taking your place in my heart. I plan on living a long life and if you'll have me, I want that life with you." Releasing his embrace, his gaze met hers one more time. She started to speak, but he placed a finger over her soft pink lips. "You don't have to say a word until I return...just don't forget there's a man across that ocean who's heart beats for you. We'll talk when I land in LA on my way home." Then, without saying another word, he turned and with a half trot, ran up the steps to the door of the plane. With one last glance over his shoulder, he paused for a moment and nodded then disappeared inside.

Strolling down the aisle toward Ben and Clay already seated in the tail section, Lou passed the colored man, his gaze shot daggers filled with hatred. But the lingering vision of Bobbie seared in his thoughts, had Lou smile at the man without a second thought, despite the fella's sour expression. Lou sat in the window seat next to Ben and joined his friends in conversation.

Ben turned toward Clay. "It won't take Teri long before she gets in with a bridge club, PTA or some such group. I guess your kids are too young for school, but your wife will make friends soon enough. She'll settle down. She just has nothing to occupy her time. In this business, it is just one of the things the wives have to get used to."

"I hope so." Clay turned toward Lou. "Did you see your buddy a couple of seats up?"

Lou glanced casually forward. Seeing the black man, he shrugged. "I still feel like a damn heel. Somehow, I can't get that altercation out of my mind. Something's not right with that boy. He's been hurt and hates the world right now."

Ben shook his head. "Come on, Lou. As far as I could see, you were too polite. If that colored fella had slammed into me, I would've probably punched him in the nose. He's been cruisin' for a brusin' since the incident in the café."

"I don't know about that. I can't help but feel like something's going on with that fella and the way he was treated today at breakfast doesn't set well. A lot of people look down their noses at blacks for the color of their skin. No one deserves that kind of berating."

Clay shook his head. "He sure is angry about something. I'd rather not mess with the man."

"It'll all come clean in the wash." Ben chuckled.

Lou frowned. "Seriously, how often must people make those men bleed for having a tan? Hell, I keep thinking of how I would feel you know…there but for the grace of God go I. I'm afraid I'd want to take revenge on the whole world."

When a voice blasted over the intercom announcing take off, the three men fastened their seatbelts. The conversation turned to business then subsided when the roar of the jets muted their voices.

Peering through a small window, Lou watched Bobbie still waiting as the jet engines thundered to a crescendo. The plane inched slowly on to the loading apron and turned toward the taxi strip then sped forward, leaving the tiny airstrip behind in a long stream of black exhaust.

Chapter Eight

Once the plane leveled off at the appropriate flight altitude, a stewardess of obvious English origin strolled down the aisle, checking on the passengers. Clay surmised her of typical British descent, pretty, tall, and she reminded him of a Welsh farm girl. He watched to see if Ben flirted as she walked by.

Ben teased her about how she clung to each seat for stability as she walked down the aisle. "What the devil have we let ourselves in for?" He leaned toward Clay as she sauntered by. "I sure hope this plane has parachutes."

The stewardess offered an icy glare. "Hard to take a bus across the ocean."

The comment stopped Ben cold. He opened his mouth, but nothing was forthcoming. Slouching into his seat, he pouted like a meek milquetoast.

Lou chuckled. "Touché."

Clay waited for him to continue the banter,

aware Ben's retort would include a mischievous quip. Before he had a chance to reply, the captain switched on the intercom.

"We are approaching the Phoenix Islands and will pass over them in a few minutes. If you look out the right-side windows, you will see the scenic aisles rising in the distance."

For a long while, Lou sat quietly, his head resting on his seatback and his eyes closed.

Clay watched the stewardess tend to her duties. He noted the vast majority of the passengers likely had past experience with long flights, but the few who demanded her attention kept her busy. An anxious woman who sat to the rear of the plane repeatedly requested water.

Clay turned in his seat and peered down the aisle.

The woman was thin, drawn, and extremely agitated. She didn't cause a scene, but he could tell she was obviously uncomfortable with flying. With a third paper cup of water, the stewardess brought the woman a miniature bottle of whiskey then sat and talked with her a few moments.

The man sitting next to Clay clenched the arm of his seat then leaned close and struck up a conversation. "I am Giovanni Cossellanei. You are American, yes?"

Clay nodded.

"The American plane, she fly so high we do not have bumps, as in our country. Is it safe we should fly so high?"

Lou glanced across the aisle. "American planes are as strong and as safe as God would will them."

60

Mr. Cossellanei shifted his gaze to Lou. "You are a God-fearing man, Mr.—?"

"Rosson, Lou Rosson."

"Yes, Mr. Rosson, I can tell by your words. You know, this trip is the first I have been in an airplane. My Rosie, she is upset I have to fly, but I tell her like you say, to have faith."

The stewardess strolled past and flashed a smile toward Lou.

Mr. Cossellanei continued his chronicle, chatting with Lou. "My Rosa, she does not realize the airplane is necessary for saving the time…"

Clay glanced outside at the thick, smoky clouds. A storm swirl darkened the clouds in the distance. An eerie chill prickled down his arms. Pulse kicking up a notch, he wondered if the flight plan sent the plane through the threatening thunderheads. Closing his eyes, his thoughts drifted as the soft hum of the engines lulled him into a nodding dose.

Outside, the weather steadily worsened. Lightning flashed and thunder rumbled as the storm encircled the plane. Captain Greg Stevens glanced at the copilot. "We need to fly above this mess. Request permission to change altitude."

The copilot nodded. "Yes, sir." He turned to the radio operator. "Contact Hawaii and request permission to change altitude to get above this storm."

Immediately, the operator flicked several switches to initiate the call then tapped out information.

After a few minutes, the copilot leaned close to Captain Stevens. "Request to change altitude granted, sir. No traffic in the area. We are authorized to take whatever course we deem expedient to avoid the storm."

"Okay Charlie, take her up to 31,000 feet and see if that will get us above this front." The passengers would note the change in altitude as the plane initiated its climb. Captain Greg reached over and switched on the seatbelt sign then pressed a tab to open the intercom microphone.

Making his voice as pleasant as possible, he announced his message. "Ladies and gentlemen, we are approaching an area of turbulence. As you might have noticed, we are changing altitude to see if we can fly above the storm. If you experience any discomfort, please bear with us. We expect to pass through this area within the next thirty minutes. Please keep your seatbelts secured until we break through the turbulence. Thank you." Flipping the switch to Off, he turned back to the controls.

Despite the change of altitude thousands of feet above the original flight plan, the rain only intensified. Thunderheads consumed the plane with an ominous, obscure veil, tossing the state-of- the-art 707 to-and-fro within its belly like a limp stuffed animal. As the flight approached the center of the storm, the aircraft shuddered and rolled. Captain Greg shot a glance through the gap between the curtains to see the luggage from the baggage compartment plunging into the aisle.

Fearful passengers screamed at the falling suitcases.

The captain veered to port, aiming the craft to fly between two towering anvil heads then swung sharply starboard. With surging jets, the plane plunged downward then staggered through opposing forces of the two monstrous cloud formations. With a blinding flash fed by the airplane's opposite polarity, a bolt of lightning cracked and lit the sky with a brilliant orange-yellow flare.

The jagged streak of lightning stabbed the starboard wingtip. A scream of metal ripping apart left the aircraft staggering in midair, responding with a sickening groan. Thrusting upward, the jet spiraled the outboard motor into the abyss with a blinding inferno. The wing abruptly sheared off inside the number four engine and folded back lazily over the top of the 707, striking the vertical stabilizer with an earth-shattering explosion.

Captain Greg cut engines one and two, then he shrieked into the intercom, "Prepare yourselves for a crash, folks. Lean as far forward in your seat as possible and put your hands over your heads."

The aircraft tilted into a sluggish turn to the right, then plummeting downward in a nauseous spin as it rapidly lost altitude. "Help me hold her nose up…I can't control her." In desperation, the captain flipped the switches to the remaining starboard engine then revved it to maximum acceleration to reverse the spin. In a downward descent, the 707 screamed like an animal in mortal pain, shaking in agony as the force of the engines exploded.

Chapter Nine

The plane rattled as it bumped and banged against air pockets.

Half in shock, Clay spun to see panic-stricken passengers. As the scene played out, time slowed, encapsulating the fear-struck terror the passengers wore within each pounding heartbeat...yet his pulse raced as their faces seared into his memory.

Mr. Cossellanei stiffened, his eyes wide and fear etched into his pale expression. He crossed his chest, muttering the Trinitarian prayer. His face gray and terrified, he lifted his gaze toward heaven. "Hail Mary, full of grace. The Lord is with the...blessed are thou..."

A panicked woman in the rear screamed for help as she fumbled madly with her seatbelt in a frantic effort to escape.

Ben's Stetson hat flew off the rack above then tumbled end-over-end past him toward the cockpit.

Baggage tumbled forward as if in a struggle to catch the rapidly receding floor. Pillows flew through the air stabbed by a mad jumble of careening objects. The entire scene gave a macabre impression of confetti, fluttering over a New York City tickertape parade.

Adrenaline pumping, Clay scanned the plane for a plan of action. Instead, his attention froze on the horror-struck travelers shrieking in terror. A jewelry box hurled from the lap of a passenger and careened forward. Clay threw his arms over his face. The chest missed him by a mere inch—but the corner clipped Ben in the temple. His head slumped forward as he collapsed against his restraining seatbelt.

Lou reached across Ben to yank him straight, but the plane twisted and spun, making the task impossible.

Blood pulsing into his face, Clay tightened his grip and yanked with all his adrenaline-infused strength until he ripped away the safety belt from its anchor. He lunged from his seat, thoughts reeling from escape...to Teri's face...to the children...and back to the plane plunging downward. He clung to whatever he could as he attempted to help screaming passengers break free...all the while mentally preparing for his own death and the inevitable trajectory.

The plane staggered out of the spin. Nose dropping, she twisted then plunged into a spiral, rotating in the opposite direction. Another anguishing shudder belched from the 707, as if the aircraft anticipated the angry waves only a scant hundred feet away, viciously awaiting the sacrifice.

For a brief moment, the nose rose as if

contemplating its final plunge into the depths. The pause gave Clay a glimmer of hope...the aircraft steadied, clinging to the air from which she belonged. He scuttled to Lou and Ben and grappled with their safety belts.

Surging waves leapt upward across the left wing and clenched the craft in a deathtrap grip. Arms protecting his head, Clay tossed down the aisle like a rag doll. To stop the momentum, he grabbed a seat and wrapped an arm around the handle, clinging for dear life then wedged his body between two seats. With wicked pleasure and brutal force, the ocean entombed the plane...sucking the cabin downward...downward...downward until the severed craft imploded, spitting out shattered fuselage to toss endlessly on the waves.

With the sudden wrench, Clay's body twisted and lurched against the side of the cabin between two seats. Dizzy and disoriented, he struggled in utter darkness. Fighting the cold rushing water, he tugged to yank free from the crimped metal pinning him against the wall.

As the plane's belly filled with salty brine, shrieks of pain and terror called for help through black obscurity.

Hands searching, Clay found where his left knee jammed into a crevice. He felt no pain, but he knew numbness below his hip meant nothing good. Bracing his leg with the wall, he kicked his free foot against the seat again and again until it gave way, then he yanked with all of his strength to free his leg.

An explosion erupted from the belly of the

aircraft…then a surge of saltwater, gurgling as it filled the cabin and swallowed the restrained passengers, dragging them down to a watery grave. Clay squeezed his eyes shut as he saw them sink beneath the surface. With little time left to escape the same fate, he turned and climbed the aisle against the gravity, tugging him downward.

A cry pierced through the darkness. "Help me." Piercing through the obscurity, Mr. Cossellanei's arm grabbed Clay's wrist. "Maria, mother of Jesus, please help me," he moaned.

Clay felt his way to the poor man's seatbelt then scratched and clawed, but the restraint held fast. A sick surge of bile rumbled into Clay's throat as he heard the agony of death claim Mr. Cossellanei. His head fell forward. Fumbling through utter blackness, Clay felt for even a weak pulse, but the old man had breathed his last. Gently laying aside the sweet Italian man's head, Clay pulled himself straight. "Lou…Ben?" He called out but heard no reply.

An ominous bubbling sounded as another surge of water seeped over his chest. Grasping the closest seat, he strained to slog away from the gushing sea. Through the abyss, he inched upward, dragging his bum leg behind him. A soft light ahead identified an escape hatch…he thrashed toward the glow.

In the midst of silent sobs beyond his reach, Clay heard Lou's weak voice.

"Ben, Clay…for God's sake, someone help me."

"Lou…thank God…where are you?" A rush of

relief scudded down his arms...one of his friends survived the crash...and he wouldn't let him drown in this hell hole tomb. Blundering through the murky oblivion, he reached through floating debris toward Lou's frantic plea...praying he'd catch hold of flesh and bone. "Lou, is that you?"

"Thank God," he murmured. "Clay. Can't move. Help."

Clay swished through the black chasm, fighting the rising water, grasping hold of whatever he could until he finally clutched Lou's shoulder. Challenging time, he prayed they could escape before the ocean sucked in and swallowed the entire plane. He reached beneath Lou's shoulders and yanked.

Lou's scream cut through the darkness with ear-shattering force.

"It's okay, buddy. What hurts? Can you tell what's wedged between you and the seat?"

"No. Oh God, just jimmy the seat."

Clay ran a hand between Lou and the area around him, searching for the obstruction. Finding nothing more than the broken seat, he leaned against the back, then hoisted his good leg above the water and kicked as hard as he could.

Lou slipped into the aisle then slid beneath the surface.

Clay lunged forward and grabbed his collar then found his shoulders. Yanking Lou's head above water, he slid his arms around the man's chest, then inched toward the glimmer of light dimly illuminating the escape hatch.

After his first involuntary scream, Lou set his jaw, clenching his lips together. Gritting his teeth, he grimly helped as much as he could between waves of pain.

The ominous rush of water grew louder and louder as the cabin filled.

With every step Clay trudged forward, Lou felt him stumble over bodies strewn haphazardly along the aisle.

Nearing the hatch, Clay lost his grip. His arm struck the jagged edge of tattered metal. Splashing forward over Lou, his body weight forced them both underwater. Thrusting an arm upward, Clay clasped hold of God only knew what, then hoisted Lou on top of his back. Again, he slogged forward. When they reached the hatch, he inspected his arm in the dim light.

Whether from shock, pain, or the sight of Clay's blood, Lou heaved.

Averting his eyes from the scarlet stain across his sleeve, Clay kicked the door, then gazed outside.

Across tossing waves, Lou saw a lifeboat bobbing up and down.

"We've got to jump, buddy. Hang on tight."

Clinging to Clay's back, Lou wondered if his friend could possibly swim to the raft with him weighing him down. "You have to leave me here, Clay. You'll never make it to the raft with me on your back."

"Not a chance. We're doing this together or not at all. I hope you can swim." Tugging Lou over his shoulder, Clay shoved him through the hatch into the ocean, then dove over him.

Lou plunged beneath the surface then stiffened to allow his body to float.

Thrusting upward, Clay emerged from beneath Lou then stretched his forearm around Lou's neck until he could grip his chin. Clay side-stroked toward the raft through pelting rain. When they were close, he stared over his shoulder at the sinking plane.

Lou followed his line of vision and glared at the jagged remnants of the jet. He could still hear the agonizing screech of severed metal as the storm lacerated the mangled cockpit...and the frantic screams of injured passengers trapped in the belly of the doomed aircraft. A gut-wrenching pain stabbed into his stomach as he watched the remaining fuselage slip beneath the surface, leaving only the tail section above the water. Acidic bile stung his throat. Swallowing hard, he squeezed his eyes shut.

Clay hoisted him higher onto his shoulders then continued his trek toward the raft.

Scanning floating debris and bodies in search of other survivors, Lou prayed to God he'd see someone still alive...but only death surrounded them.

When they reached the lifeboat, Clay secured Lou by hooking his arms over the rubbery edge, then he hoisted himself aboard. Once safe in the boat, he gripped Lou under his arms and tugged until he could grasp hold of his body and haul him into the raft.

Racked with pain, Lou rolled onto his back.

Clay adjusted his torso and helped Lou

straighten his body. Then, at a sudden splash, Clay spun around.

Lou twisted his neck to see another arm hook over the side of the raft. Thank God. At least one other passenger survived.

Chapter Ten

C lay dove forward. He clasped the man's wrist to keep him from slipping under water. Drawing on what little strength he had left, he yanked the man's shirt and hauled him aboard.

Blood gushing from a cut over one brow, James collapsed against the side of the raft. He raised his face toward the sky. Eyes closed, he held the position while the rain rinsed away the salt and jet fuel.

Clay shifted his attention to his friend. Pale and drawn, Lou writhed, his breathing harsh and irregular. Inspecting him from head to foot, Clay searched for external bleeding but saw nothing.

He examined his own body for injuries. Aside from the gash on his left bicep, he noticed a splotch of crimson on his wrist. Running a finger over the stain, he realized the blood wasn't his own and flashed a stare toward James.

Blood still trickled from the man's forehead. He lay limp against the side of the raft.

"You okay?" Clay called out.

The black man turned his head to face Clay then glared. "Do you really care?"

Clay rolled his eyes then returned his attention to Lou. Taking off his jacket, he rolled the fabric then lifted his friend's head and positioned the coat under his neck.

A metallic groan belched from the plane, and Clay spun toward the sound. With a final farewell, the tail briefly shuddered then majestically descended below the surface.

Scorched remnants from the flight littered the sea. Beyond the debris, Clay caught site of another raft. Through smoke and drizzle, he couldn't tell for sure how many survivors made it aboard, but he made out at least two distinct figures. His gaze drifted to the water surrounding his immediate area. He searched for some sign of life. All he saw were shadows of those who perished, suspended by lingering pockets of air just beneath the surface. Of the ninety-seven passengers plus the crew, he could identify only five survivors. He considered trying to connect with the other raft, but jagged shrapnel and debris lay between them. Joining the others held little benefit if the wreckage pierced this lifeboat. A shiver ran down his back as he lowered his gaze.

An oil slick bubbled to the surface a few yards away…then another until the sea splattered with tiny patches. Some exploded into a fleeting blaze of fire then fizzled as heaving waves separated the fuel from the splintered tanks. A lone life jacket floated by. How lucky he was to survive. Now, they drifted with no destination through chaos. Pelting rain tossed them against the angry ocean.

James gazed into the water and scooped up a small doll dressed in oil-sodden rags. Her black hair hung forlorn and matted. Her tattered muumuu was soiled beyond repair.

The doll reeked of jet fuel strong enough for Clay to smell, but James tucked the doll next to him then stared across the ocean.

The storm, not satisfied with its violent rage, rumbled in the distance.

Clay turned to Lou and inspected him closer. Stomach swollen and bulging, he showed definite signs of broken ribs, compounded by internal bleeding. Having no medical training, Clay knew little more than common sense about injury care. He secured Lou as best he could and tried to make him comfortable. Eventually, Lou fell into a fitful sleep.

Finally, the wind subsided, stealing the rain as it blew toward the north and leaving behind a single dinghy filled with water adrift through the dense fog.

Focused on his friend, Clay lost sight of the other raft. He leaned against the side of the tiny boat. His hands numbed from the cold water. Exhausted by the entire ordeal, he knew he needed rest, but he saw no alternative than to bail the rainwater. They had to keep the raft afloat. He braced his right leg against the fold in the rubber then bent and shoved water over the side. With only his hands to bail, he was pleasantly surprised when James silently joined him, heaving water over the opposite side.

After what seemed like hours of bailing, Clay heard Lou shriek out in a panic.

"Ben? Sweet Jesus, Clay, we left Ben in the plane."

Clay immediately halted his water removal and scuttled toward Lou to calm his angst, but by the time he reached his friend, Lou had drifted into unconsciousness once again.

Unaffected by the others, James continued to bail. Clay checked the contents of the disaster compartment affixed to the side of the raft and found a medical kit, some concentrated rations, a small canteen of water, and an emergency radio. He glanced toward Lou, still tossing in a restless slumber. Laying the kit to one side, he chose the radio and studied the device. Moments later, he anchored the base in his lap and began cranking to emit an SOS signal.

Occasionally glancing toward James, he wondered what had the man in such a rage. Regardless of their differences, they were stuck with each other for only God knew how long. He hoped they could at least find a way to be civil.

A gentle breeze blew the raft through the fog toward an unknown destination, while three men, drained by their nightmare, struggled to survive. One way or another, they would learn what was needed as problems arose...hour upon hour, and day upon day, as they remained adrift in the hands of fate.

Chapter Eleven

T he rhythmic up and down sway lulled the survivors into sleep—until the first light of dawn. James blinked awake and stared at a crystal blue sky. After two days of pelting rain, this was the first sunlight he'd seen since the crash. Thankful the rain had finally cleared, he relished in the warmth of the sun beating down on his back. A groan from the far side of the raft reminded him he was not alone. He twisted toward his two companions.

Lou lay restless, mumbling incoherently. His body jerked as if he was in a lot of pain.

Crawling to his knees, James edged toward the first aid box, hoping to find something to help the poor man sleep better. Reaching for the kit, his knee slid and the movement to catch himself shot a stabbing pain through his forehead and broke-open the cut over his eye. The tempest of anger seething just below the surface shot to the forefront. He snatched the kit and drew it to his chest then eased himself downward against the side of the raft. He shuffled aside bandages in search of something to stop the bleeding. Finding sulfur powder, he chose some gauze and a bandage, then tended to his injury.

Once he finished, he studied the contents. He moved aside a salve for burns, some aspirin, and a few other items before grabbing the small bottle from the side pocket. He read the label. Morphine. He glanced at Lou then back to the white tablets and paused. At first, it rankled him to help a white man...but something about this particular man felt different. He shook his head to dismiss the sentiment weakening his rebellious resolve and returned the bottle to the kit.

Again, Lou groaned.

Clenching his jaw, James snatched the kit then slid toward Lou. Prying off the morphine lid, he took out two tablets then recapped the bottle and tossed it into the bag. He reached for the canteen then stared at Lou and slid an arm under the man's head, lifting it slightly.

Lou opened his eyes a slit and peered at James through his sticky lashes.

"Are you in pain?" James whispered.

Lou offered a weak nod.

"Here, these will help." James dropped the pills into Lou's slightly opened mouth then held the canteen to his lips to help him swallow. He gently released Lou's head against the raft then twisted to return the canteen to its place. As he crept down the edge of the raft, he noticed Clay begin to stir.

Stretching, Clay turned toward Lou, then

stiffened. "Hey, boy, leave him alone." Clay spit out. He eyed James then stared at the first aid kit sitting beside him. "What the hell do you think you're doing?"

"No… Clay… please." Lou's words came out slow and weak.

Clay scrambled to his feet and made his way to Lou. "Are you alright?"

Lou's weak voice muffled, but his face showed intent. "He helped. Gave me morphine for pain."

James snarled at Clay but said nothing. Grabbing the first aid kit, he snatched the bandages, dipped a piece of gauze over the side to dampen it, then ripped the blood-soaked dressing from his forehead and tossed it into the water.

"You fool. You want to bring every shark in the area to our raft? They're attracted to blood."

Rolling his eyes, James swiped across his wound, then fashioned a new dressing. Maybe Clay was right, but his judgement didn't help the ethnic feud silently seething between them. James scooted across the raft and returned the medical kit to a secure spot.

After talking with Lou quietly for a few seconds, Clay left his side and scooted toward James. "Sorry. I thought…never mind. Can I help you with your bandage? You can't see to clean it properly."

"Get away from me, whitey." His voice fumed with rage.

Clay's hands fell to his side. Clasping them tightly, he gazed toward Lou then back to James. "Look, you must realize I didn't know—"

"Right." Again, James sneered.

Clay spoke again, but his voice trailed off. Still sitting, he paused for a long beat then turned away and crawled toward Lou.

James pressed the bandage against his forehead to add pressure to his wound, only releasing it long enough to check his blood flow. After repeating the process several times, he sprinkled the cut with sulfur then applied a clean bandage and taped the gauze to his forehead. From the corner of his eye, he could see Clay still staring at him.

After watching James for several long moments, he turned his back and rifled through his pockets. Finding a handkerchief, he scrubbed it in saltwater, then rung out the excess. He scrambled to Lou and washed the grime from his face and hands. After completing the task, he rinsed the cloth, then ran it over himself.

Realizing Clay watched his every move, James raised an eyebrow and wondered what other activity Clay might follow. Feeling bulges in his rear pockets, he drew out a waterlogged billfold and set it on its side to dry. Finding his cigarettes in a sodden package, he opened the pack and carefully placed them beside the billfold one by one. He felt his breast pocket and found a pack of matches then placed them beside the other treasures. Fashioning a crevice to shield them from splashing waves and the light breeze, he left everything to dry, then tossed a stare at Lou before snatching the radio and taking on the laborious cranking job.

Lou raised a hand and patted his own breast pocket and the movement caught Jim's attention.

"I hope those matches will light once they dry." Lou gazed at them critically. "I sure could use a cigarette."

James nodded. "We'll see."

Lou snapped his fingers. "Hey. I might have some dry matches." He dug into his pants pocket and drew out a pocket secretary, now soiled into a gloppy mess, some small lumps of mangled papers, and matches equally as wet. Reaching into his breast pocket, he drew out a cigarette case and smiled when he saw his smokes were seemingly dry. "These will work if we can find a light."

Clay checked the storage area and searched the pockets but came up empty-handed. "Nothing here." He shrugged.

Still cranking the radio, James watched Clay with a malevolent gaze.

Clay scuttled back to Lou. "You hungry?"

Lou shook his head. Shifting his position slightly, he winced and groaned. After a long moment of holding his breath, he called to James. "You're welcome to have one of my cigarettes when the matches dry."

James shoved a hand in his pocket and withdrew a lighter. He turned it slowly in his hand, letting it gleam in the sunlight. When Clay glanced up. James tossed him the lighter, deliberately aiming just short of his target.

Clenching his jaw, Clay shifted his gaze to Lou. As if reading his friend's mind, he slowly reached down, picked up the lighter, then flipped it several times. He was rewarded for his efforts, when a small blue flame flickered in the breeze...but it quickly died. Clay picked up a dry cigarette and put it to his lips. This time, shielding the flame with cupped hands, he bent down and grabbed a light. After drawing in the smoke deeply, he held out the cigarette and gave it to Lou. Then he reached across the raft and handed the lighter to James. "Thanks." Taking another cigarette from the pack, he lit it from Lou's, then offered the pack to James. "You want a smoke?"

James pressed his lips together and continued cranking.

Clay shrugged. "Suit yourself. I tried." He drew in a long puff then blew out several smoke rings. "Look, Mr. X...James, or whatever the hell you call yourself, we are in this hell together. We damn well had no choice of companions. If we had, I'm sure you wouldn't have chosen me. So, as long as we have to rely on each other, it would be a hell of a lot smarter and more palatable if we were at least courteous, especially considering Lou's condition. Don't you agree?"

James paused and glared at Clay. He took one of his sundried cigarettes and lit the end, then blew out a stream of smoke and savored the taste but said nothing.

Again, Clay rolled his eyes and turned away.

Lou breathed out a long sigh. "Do either of you really know why you harbor such rage against each other?" He frowned and turned to Clay. "Attitudes aside, Jim has done nothing but help us since he crawled into this raft. If his skin was lily-white, would you treat him with the same righteous indignation?"

Clay grimaced and lowered his chin like a pouting child.

Lou pinched his brows together and shifted his gaze toward James. "And you, Jim...I can see you carry a lot of hostility toward white folks...and I don't doubt your motives are justified, but do you not see that condemning an entire race makes you no better than those responsible for your pain?"

Jim leaned back onto his calves then wiped the sweat from his brow with his arm. "Burn me once, shame on you...burn me twice, shame on me. I'm tired of being burned."

Lou ran a hand through his hair then shifted positions and winced. "I don't suspect your daddy taught you to quit...did he?"

Jim turned and gazed across the endless ocean. His father, rest his soul, would have pushed him to run the course regardless of the hurtles he met.

"No reply necessary, Jim." Lou reached for a wooden paddle then tugged himself straight, but a sudden surge of pain caught him off guard and he let out a tortured groan.

Immediately, both men lunged toward him to help, but halted when Lou held up a hand. "I'm okay—but if you two don't find a way to work together...take a good look around you. There's no one else in sight to help us." He pushed his fists against the bottom of the raft and slid into a more comfortable position. "I'm useless...but you two— together—have a fighting chance to keep us all alive...at least long enough to be rescued...or find land." He shook his head. "But divided...we all die."

Clay stared at Jim, his gaze shooting daggers.

Jim glared a return stare then leaned against the side of the raft and gazed toward the horizon. "The wind has picked up a bit. It's still sunny now, but from the looks of those thunderheads in the distance, we might get more rain sooner than later."

Clay lifted his gaze skyward then glanced around the small raft. "There's a canvas tucked into the crease behind you, Jim."

Jim turned and made his way to the rear of the raft. Grasping hold of the tarp, he shook it loose and inspected the material then scanned the edge of the lifeboat. "The canvas snaps to the sides." He hitched his chin to the opposite side. "There's a collapsed pole over there that must support the middle." Kneeling, he attached the canvas to the edge of the raft.

Bum left leg dragging, Clay scuttled toward Jim, snatched a corner of the canvas and snapped the opposite side then shoved the pole inside a notch in the middle of the raft, creating a shelter that covered the entire vessel. When he finished, he turned to face Jim. "Hand me the SOS radio. I'll crank for a while."

Noting Clay's attempted olive branch—if only for Lou's sake—Jim handed him the radio then gazed toward his injured companion. He wasn't sure what to think of the man, but Lou sure had guts to stand up to the two men who held his life in their hands.

Jim crawled to the back of the raft and stretched out his legs. Staring into the vast ocean, he wondered if they'd find land before their food or water ran out. And what would become of Lou if he couldn't get medical help? Though he shed little blood, Jim could tell his internal injuries were more serious than a few broken ribs. The bruises around his chest suggested massive internal bleeding.

Jim searched for land along the horizon but saw nothing but the endless ocean. Turning to face Clay, he considered Lou's questions. Jim spent a lifetime trying to prove himself…to fit into the white man's world. But at every turn, his efforts were met with disdain. He didn't start this battle…but he sure as hell wanted to end it.

Still, Lou's argument made sense. Fighting fire with fire only intensified the inferno…could Jim have been wrong to follow Malcom's solution? What if violence only increased the division…the hatred and rage between Blacks and Whites?

In theory, Lou's viewpoint held water. But Jim's experience taught him something entirely different. He shook his head. After six-hundred-eighteen documented deaths in the Civil War, a promise of equality was realized. But a hundred years later, skin color still determined a man's worth. Jim knew firsthand the damage decades of vitriol now plagued the nation. How could anyone expect change after generations of parent-to-child indoctrination and hostility had taken root?

He watched Clay churn the radio handle for close to an hour before he relieved him, and so the task went, alternating cranking, while the other man rested, but neither spoke during the exchange.

85

Chapter Twelve

A fter wandering through several shops, including a jewelry store and her new favorite dress shop, Teri made her way toward the grocery store. Strolling through big double doors, she grabbed a cart and placed her purse in the baby seat then perused the store, choosing her list items along the way and pausing momentarily to read the magazine headlines.

The check-out counter had only one woman in line, so she waited, gazing lazily through the front window. A crowd congregating in the front of the store drew her attention. After paying her bill, she lifted the sack of groceries and walked outside, still curious about the group collecting. She edged closer, craning her neck to observe what caused the commotion.

At a sudden shattering of glass, she spun...then collapsed onto the sidewalk. Her groceries dropped to the ground, splattering broken eggs and milk over the scattered food and walkway. She squeezed her eyes shut.

Face burning, she lifted a hand to her cheek. Sharp needles ripped at her fingers and a warm, sticky substance dribbled down her arm. Opening her eyes a slit, she saw a blur of images hovering over her. Why were they staring? She slid a hand downward and tugged at her skirt to be sure it covered her bare legs.

Attempting to rise, she caught a glimpse of her hand drenched in scarlet. A swirl of vertigo then nausea enveloped her. She crumpled to the ground in excruciating pain until a cold darkness consumed her. In the distance, the wail of an ambulance moaned, and voices droned above.

A stranger knelt beside her. "You'll be all right, honey. Just lie still. The ambulance is on the way."

What did the woman mean? Was she talking to me?

A stab of adrenaline clenched her neck, shooting prickly waves down her arms and legs. Surrounded by hovering figures whispering against a stir of chaos in the background, she focused on their discourse to help her understand what happened.

"Oh Lord…so much blood."

Blood? Drifting in and out of consciousness, she felt her heart throb from beneath her face, pulsating in unison with the pounding in her chest. The piercing pain took her breath away. And she didn't want to hear those awful voices whispering above.

"Do you suppose she's dead?"

"Did you see her face? It looked just awful, all bloody and covered with shattered glass."

"Poor little thing, she was so pretty."

"What a pity."

"Did anyone see what happened?"

"I sure did. When that young fella threw a can through the window, the darn thing exploded and spit shattered glass everywhere. The shards flew directly into that poor woman's face."

"Step aside, folks I'm a doctor." A man bent over her. Again, blackness shrouded her, but this time she couldn't fight her way back. In the distance, fading muttering hushed as her world went silent.

Officer Harry Johnson glanced at the physician attending the victim and decided to gather her information when they got to the hospital. He held up a hand and forcefully corralled the crowd then drew out his notepad and pencil. "Okay. Everyone, calm down and tell me what you saw one at a time."

A middle-aged man stepped forward. "I saw the whole incident from my bakery shop window. A colored boy held up a vegetable can and slung it smack-dab at the grocery store. The glass shattered, shooting slivers everywhere, and that young woman was standing directly in the path."

"Name?" The officer tapped his pencil on the pad.

"Arthur Campbell. I own the bakery next door. If that boy had come in and stolen from me, he wouldn't be walking."

A woman chimed in. "As I approached the

store, I saw the owner leaning on the wall having a smoke. When the boy stepped outside, he musta seen the owner, too, 'cause he took off running...but the owner nabbed him. The food he stole fell from under his jacket to the ground...all except one can he caught in his hand...he gazed downward at that can and his stare was as if he was surprised to see the can clenched in his grip. A second later, he lobbed it straight at the window."

"Name, ma'am?"

"Susan Weiland."

He jotted down the information.

"Those coloreds are all alike. Savages, the lot of them," one old lady yelled out.

Officer Johnson scowled at her comment and shook his head. The attitude of those holier-than-thou, uppity, bigots irked his soul. "The boy stole food, for God's sake, lady. Not a diamond ring."

"Well, I never." She turned toward the crowd. "Did you ever see anyone so rude in your life?" She huffed then scurried off.

"Break it up now. Move along." Johnson shoved past the crowd and strode toward the store, leaving the bystanders to their gossip. At the sound of a siren screaming, he threw a glance over his shoulder toward the road to see the approaching ambulance. They'd transport her to the hospital in short order. He needed to hurry if he wanted to meet them there.

After a quick interview with the store owner, he rushed to his patrol car. The spectators were right about one thing, that woman's injuries were serious. He'd seen a lot over the past twenty years, and the damage to her face was right up there with the worst.

When he arrived at the emergency receiving area, he rushed inside to see a nurse evaluating the injured woman. He needed to find out who the victim was, along with her prognosis, so he could notify her next of kin.

The patient moaned and mumbled unintelligibly, while brilliant red stains seeped onto the stark white sheets stretched over the gurney.

Bending low to hear what the woman mumbled, the nurse dropped her gaze, then stood and shook her head.

Chapter Thirteen

R ob Robinson frowned at the demanding telephone ring sounding from his secretary's desk.

Sally finished tapping on her typewriter before answering the call. "Smith Robinson and Company. May I help you?"

"This is Officer Harry Johnson. I'm at Houston General Hospital. There's been an accident, and I'm trying to get in touch with Mr. Emery Clayton."

"I'm sorry, officer. Mr. Clayton is out of town on business." She gazed at her boss now standing beside her desk.

"May I please speak with your employer? This is an emergency."

"One moment, please." The secretary pushed one of the buttons at the base of the phone then peered toward Mr. Robinson. "I assume you heard."

"Yes. I'll pick up the call in my office." He walked a few steps then shot a glance over his

93

shoulder. "I'll keep my door open. Let me know immediately when you finish that letter." Robinson stepped into the next room and ground out his cigar in the amber ashtray on his desk then picked up the phone. "Robinson here."

"Mr. Robinson, this is Officer Harry Johnson. I'm at Houston General Hospital, and I'm trying to reach Mr. Emery Clayton. His wife has been injured. Could you tell us how we can reach him?"

"I'm sorry, officer. It's impossible to get a hold of Mr. Clayton at this point. He is in flight on his way to Australia. How badly is Mrs. Clayton hurt?"

"I'm not a physician, sir, but from what I saw, her injuries were extensive."

"You tell the doctor to do whatever is necessary for Mrs. Clayton and spare no expense. Our firm will take care of the bill."

"Mrs. Clayton is quite concerned about her children. They are due home from school shortly and will have no one to care for them. She asked if you would mind dropping by the hospital to grab her keys and perhaps watch over the children until her parents arrived from out of town."

"Tell her not to worry. We will handle everything. My wife can pick up the children and bring them to our home."

Officer Johnson gave Rob the Clayton's address then thanked him. "I'll tell the physician you'll be by shortly for the keys."

Dropping the receiver into its cradle, he yelled to his secretary, disregarding the intercom, "Sally, get on the phone and send a wire to Mr. Clayton's hotel in Australia. Don't scare the man to death but make sure he understands he's needed here as soon as possible. His wife was in an accident and was badly injured."

A moment later, he was on the phone again. "Meg? Emery Clayton's wife was hurt in an accident. His kids are due home from school. Drop whatever you're doing and get to his house before they reach the door. Just wait with them until I can get there with a key. Sweetheart, they'll need to stay at our house for a while...until Teri's parents arrive from Georgia. Is that okay with you?"

"Oh my. How awful. Of course, Rob." Meg asked for the address and promised to leave immediately. Rob stood and paced to the rack for his coat and hat. As he left, he called to his secretary, "Sally, I'm on my way to the hospital. If anyone calls or wants me for any reason, tell them I can't be reached."

Rob hurried to his car and hopped inside. His mind focused on what needed to be done in Clay's absence. Feeling rushed and worried, he picked up his speed, keeping a close eye in the rearview mirror for police.

Bobbie waved at Jeri and Jan, two stewardess friends lingering by a plane, chitchatting with the copilot. The sun shone high in the sky and the wings on her cap and pockets glistened as they caught the sparkling rays. Smiling, she thought of the day ahead. She planned to go uptown and buy the blue jersey dress she'd seen in the shop window a few days earlier. The aqua color reminded her of the ocean at the secluded white coral beach where she and Lou spent the afternoon...the memory seared into her mind...the grove of palm trees...the warm summer sun...the soft breeze gently swaying the palms...the tiny whitecaps tossing to-and-fro across the surface...and his kiss.

The blue-green dress was perfect for her date with Lou. She envisioned herself wearing the frock, dancing with Lou, the fabric swaying like the palms as he twirled her around the floor. He'd love how the dipped neckline would showoff the locket he bought for her. Though the gown cost quite a bit more than she should spend, she could cut corners on meals for a week or two to make up the difference.

Rushing toward the ramp, she made her way into the administration building then turned toward operations to file her report. Gathering her ticket stubs, she picked up a flight report then sat to fill out the papers. The large room, typically buzzing with activity, was oddly quiet. She gazed around. No one else was in the office except the duty officer and radio engineer. The usual flurry of flight crews and stewardesses were nowhere to be seen. She shrugged and smiled, pleased she chose the perfect time to fill out her report. Now, she could catch the next limousine into town with no waiting at all.

After completing the paperwork, she gathered together the pages, pushed back her chair, and stood then paced toward the duty officer to hand in her reports.

He accepted her proffer and checked the

sheets.

With a vague sense of foreboding, Bobbie stared at his mechanical movements.

He lifted his gaze from the papers. "You haven't heard, have you, Bobbie?"

"Heard what?" His solemn stare sent a chill down her arms, and she rubbed them in response.

"Greg's overdue...and there's a crash notice on the bulletin board."

A knot formed in her throat and she caught her breath. "Oh, no! Who is with him?" Tears stung her eyes as they pressed to escape.

His reply was stoic. "Charlie...Scott Bilo...Sue Parker...and the Marshall twins."

Without speaking, Bobbie turned from the duty officer and wandered into the flight crew's lounge toward the bulletin board. Her breath still catching, she gazed at the notice.

She'd dated Charlie briefly...or maybe she should say they went out a few times. He was a happy-go-lucky sort of fellow. She often saw Greg's wife around the flight lounge...a small, dark little woman whose world revolved around Greg. A prayer raced through her thoughts and she whispered it aloud, "Please Lord, let them be all right."

Staring at the notice, she tried to read, but unshed tears blurred the words. She brushed them away with the back of her hand.

Flight 217 reported turbulence over the Pacific Ocean.
No further information. Plane

presumed down.
Search efforts prevented from a
rescue mission due to extreme
weather conditions.

She felt the blood drain from her face, and her cheeks numbed. "No. Dear God. No. Lou was on that plane, too." An icy rock froze in the pit of her stomach. Clenching the edge of the bulletin board, she bowed her head and bit at her lip, waiting for the hollow feeling exhausting her energy to pass. The soft, burnished gleam of the locket around her neck caught her eye. Placing a hand on the cold, gold heart, she forced a breath into her lungs then staggered to a chair and crumpled into the seat.

She had known Lou for such a short time, but she knew she loved him deeply. She envisioned his handsome face and memorized his eyes, but she had no picture to remind her. Lou was gone. "No," she belted out, not caring who heard her cry. Her mind rejected the thought. The plane was only presumed down. Maybe the radio failed. How many times had she heard of that happening?

The stewardesses with whom she shared the last leg of her flight entered the room and called out. "Hey, Bobbie, want something from the snack bar?"

Gazing at them blankly, she shook her head. Then, allowing the question to register, she yelled, "Coffee, please. Black."

Jeri and Jan returned with three steaming cups and handed one to Bobbie then sat.

"You've heard, haven't you? It's just terrible.

Any of us could have been on that flight."

Both women knew Bobbie had dated Charlie.

Jan reached for Bobbie's hand. "The duty officer just told us. He heard the SOS."

"They'll be able to get out shortly to pick up the survivors." Jeri's voice was laced with hope. "The weather is breaking now."

Bobbie knew the conditions and the slim possibility of survivors. "Two rafts and how many passengers?"

Jan answered tentatively, "About a hundred-fifty."

"A hundred-fifty?" Jeri stared into her coffee.

The three sat silently, each wrapped in her own thoughts.

Others entered the flight lounge and conversations concerning the flight buzzed.

Bobbie drained her cup and stood. "I need to go...now." She turned and ambled to the locker-room. Leaning over the sink, she filled her hands with cold water, then held them to her face. Yanking a paper towel, she rubbed her face and hands.

Jan pushed open the door and stepped toward Bobbie. "Are you okay?"

"No...but I will be."

"I thought you and Charlie just went out for laughs. I had no idea he meant that much to you."

"It wasn't Charlie, Jan. I'm upset over a passenger on the flight."

"Do you need to talk? We can grab a bite to eat."

"No, thanks. I think I'll wait around here for a

little while until they find out more about the crash."

"Alright. If you need anything—"

"I'm okay, Jan. But thanks."

She nodded, then left.

Bobbie waited for hours, but still no news arrived. Exhausted, she took a cab into town. Strolling by the dress shop, she teared up when she saw the beautiful chiffon dress she planned to buy for her upcoming date with Lou. Stepping to the curb, she haled a taxi without waiting for the bus she usually took. When the cabbie stopped at her apartment building, she handed him her fare. Thoughts spinning around the day she spent with Lou, she mindlessly checked for mail in her box then trudged upstairs. Halfway down the hallway, she fumbled in her purse for her keys.

The woman in the next apartment poked her head outside the door to see who was rattling around, but seeing Bobbie, the woman withdrew without speaking.

Bobbie pushed open the door and closed it behind her. She hung her coat and placed her hat on the shelf then kicked off her shoes. She stumbled into the living room and sprawled out on the couch, praying she would escape into sleep to drown the torturous images she had of Lou as the plane plunged into the ocean.

"Your neighbor let me in," Jeri whispered.

Bobbie spun her head to see her friend standing behind the chair. An ashtray in hand, she held out a fresh cigarette. "I told her it was a matter of life and death I talk with you."

"Was it?" Bobbie asked. She took the cigarette and drew in a long drag. She came home to be alone. The last thing she needed was to talk.

"I saw Jan on my way out."

"Oh?"

The radio was tuned low. Obviously, Jeri was listening for news. "She said you knew a passenger on the flight and teased about you being crazy for him." Jeri lit another cigarette and took a puff.

"And what did you say?"

"I told her to shut up, and I came directly here." She plopped down in the chair. "Are you—"

"Am I upset? Worried? Angry? Scared?"

"I know you must be all of those things…but are you in love with him?"

Bobbie dropped her gaze to the floor, attempting to hold back tears threatening to burst. Afraid if she cried, she couldn't stop, she changed the subject. "Have you heard any news yet?"

"No, nothing, just the first report of the crash. You?"

"No." Bobbie stood and silently padded into her tiny kitchenette. She snatched two green coffee mugs from pegs under the cabinets and poured two stiff shots of bourbon then reached in the freezer and took out an ice tray. After dropping a cube in each cup, she replaced the tray, brought the cups into the living room, and handed one to Jeri.

After taking a stiff drink, Jeri spoke. "The way you took the news of the crash, I knew you were upset over more than Charlie…are you in love with your passenger?"

Bobbie's gaze met Jeri's. In her own misery,

101

she could think of nothing to say except the truth. "Yes," she whispered and lifted her drink. As she took another swig, the floodgates opened, and all her pent-up emotions released. "I'm madly and crazy in love with Lou. We haven't known each other long, but somehow, we both knew…we felt an unmistakable connection and—"

A bulletin sounded with an urgent tone as the radio station released a breaking news report. Both girls turned toward the radio and stared.

Bobbie's heart froze. She couldn't breathe. Dreading to hear the facts, she squeezed her eyes tightly and hoped against hope the news would be good and not her worst nightmare.

Chapter Fourteen

R ob peeked into the hospital room to see the patient sleeping on the bed in the recovery room, moaning softly as she struggled toward consciousness. The nurse stood quietly and edged closer to Teri. After checking her pulse, she straightened the covers then slipped outside the door. "Mr. Robinson, she's stirring and will be waking up soon. You can go in for a few minutes, but please…don't say anything that might upset her. She's not dealing well with her injuries, so, for the time being, keep everything positive. If you need me, I'll be at the nurses' desk."

Rob tiptoed as he entered the room and peered around the corner toward Teri.

Her eyes opened a slit.

Edging forward, he stared at her dark hair peeking from beneath the edges of the massive bandages covering her head and face. Lying there in the sterile bed, she looked so young and vulnerable. "Are you awake?" he whispered.

She let out a soft moan.

"I can only stay a few moments, Teri. Please, don't try to talk. I just want you to know Meg picked up the children from school and brought them to our house. They are doing just fine."

Teri forced slurred words. "Wh... what... ha... happened to... me?"

"Shattered glass from the grocery store window cut your face. But you'll be just fine. The doctor assured me your wounds are clean and there's little danger of infection."

"I...Clay... need Clay—"

"Don't worry. Clay will be back as soon as he can catch a flight. You need to rest, now. I'll be back later, then we can talk."

She lowered her gaze then closed her eyes.

Rob stood still and watched her a moment, then tiptoed out the door. When he reached the elevator, he pushed the down button and waited, imagining how horrible it would be to see Meg lying in a hospital bed with wounds like Teri. *Clay will be devastated when he hears the news.* When the elevators separated, two interns stood before Rob, talking about a case. They flew past him without so much as a glance.

When he stepped inside and pressed the main floor button, the elevator closed, then jerked, descending with a mechanical flushing noise. The moment he stepped outside, he drew in the crisp, fresh air, filling his lungs to dispel the cloying odor of anesthesia then paced toward his car. Mentally noting to have Sally send flowers to Teri, he started the engine and checked his mirror.

The radio, tuned to news, beeped a special report warning. What now? Rob lowered his gaze and turned up the volume.

"Just breaking, Eastern Airlines flight 217 from Honolulu, Hawaii, to Sydney, Australia, crashed into the Pacific Ocean. The flight, carrying over one-hundred fifty passengers and crew, reported strong turbulence and requested a change in altitude shortly before the towers lost contact. Search and rescue teams recovered evidence of the downed plane. No survivors have been discovered. Captain Greg Stevens, his crew, and all passengers are presumed dead. In other news…"

Stunned, Rob reached for the ignition key and turned off the engine. He sat silently, overcome by the news report. He had no need to check Clayton's flight schedule. He knew the manifest would include his employee…his friend's name. Rob had booked the flight… and now, his employee… his friend was dead.

On the fourth floor of Houston General Hospital, Teri Clayton drifted in and out of a fitful sleep, stirring only when awakened for medicinal purposes. Afternoons became evenings and the small room danced with shadows and distant memories. Morphine quelled the pounding pain in her head and the fiery sting burning her face, but an ache in her heart deepened with loneliness. Sadness shrouded her with a veil of indifference…and a noise, a light, or a prick of pain faded into the blessed darkness surrounding her once more.

What felt like weeks and months droned on, and she slept. The cold, sterile odor the hospital exuded sickened her stomach. At times, she wondered if the smell emanated from her own wounds...or was it the stench of death consuming her. Thoughts of Clay kept her from dwelling on her accident...but where was he? Why hadn't he come to see her?

This morning, Teri awakened at the sound of nurses shuffling down the hallway. A rap sounded before the door creaked open. A nurse poked her head inside and smiled when she saw Teri's gaze shift toward her voice. She waddled into the room, poured some water in a bowl then, with a warm cloth, she washed the unbandaged areas of Teri's face.

"My, but we do look better this morning. We'll get you all cleaned up then Dr. Morgan wants to take a quick look to see how you're healing. I have to say you had us worried for a while, but now that Doctor Morgan eased up on your medication, you're coming alive again."

Teri scooted upward, but the effort accomplished little more than a rush of pain.

"Here, hun. Let me help you sit." The nurse fluffed the pillow and cranked her bed up slightly, so she bent at the waist. "You must be tired of laying down all the time. Maybe Dr. Morgan will let you sit by the window in the sunshine for a bit."

Teri's head throbbed, but as long as she stayed still, the intensity dulled.

After taking her vitals, cleaning and changing the top sheet and blanket, the nurse briefly stepped into the hallway and returned with a magazine and two books. "I thought you might enjoy these. A patient left them a few days ago, and nobody has asked for them." She set the books on the bedside table then faced Teri. "You do like to read, don't you?"

Teri feigned a half-smile then realized the bandages hid her facial expressions. "Yes." She squeaked out the hoarse reply. "Thank you, Nurse Williams."

"You're welcome. Call me Stella, hun. I have to tend to the other patients, but if you need anything, you just let us know." She scuffed into the hallway and disappeared into the bustle of hospital activity.

Teri glanced at the *LOOK* magazine, then read the title of the two books, *To Kill A Mockingbird* by Harper Lee and *Goldfinger* by Ian Fleming. She chose the Harper Lee book, if for no other reason than the cover. A rose held in the teeth of a skeleton head gave her the willies, so she shoved aside *Goldfinger* and opened *To Kill A Mockingbird*. Leafing past the title page and dedication, she found chapter one and began to read.

"When he was nearly thirteen, my brother—"

The doctor strode into her room without knocking. "Well, well. It's nice to see you sitting, Mrs. Clayton. I'm Dr. Morgan." He glanced at her chart then, laying it aside, he pulled up a chair and straddled the seat. "How are you feeling?"

Teri shrugged, hoping the doctor would tell her

how she was progressing and when she might be released to go home.

"I'll bet you have a lallapalooza of a headache. You're mighty lucky you got off as easily as you did." He reached for her wrist and held it for a minute to take her pulse. "Do you remember what happened...why you're here in the hospital?"

Teri nodded.

"The glass shattered, and shards flew directly at your face. We spent hours in surgery taking out every piece. The one in your right eye was of most concern."

Her hand flew to her face. Only then did she realize the extent of the bandages. "How long will it take for my eye to heal?" Again, her voice came out horse and raspy."

"With any luck, the damaged eye will heal enough for you to see, but your vision might be impaired. We'll see when the bandages come off."

Her hand slid from her face to her throat, and she gazed at the doctor with a pleading eye.

"Your throat was injured as well, but it's healing nicely, and your voice should return over time."

She dropped her gaze to the crisp white sheet. *Over time? What did that even mean?* Would she be able to see enough to drive, or sing lullabies to her children? And what about scars? Would she be disfigured...grotesque?

Doctor Morgan crooked a finger and raised her chin. "Hey now, no sulking. You've had an awful accident, but you're getting stronger every day. These things take time to heal, so you need to be patient." He stood and edged toward the door. "Are you hungry?"

Again, Teri shrugged.

"I would think by now you'd be ready for some solid food. I'll have the nurse bring you something easy to swallow. How about some oatmeal?" Without waiting for an answer, he continued. "If you're not in too much pain, I'd like to cut back on your morphine."

She widened her good eye. "Morphine?"

"Just enough to take the edge off of your pain. Is that okay?"

Placing a hand on her throat, she forced her voice. "When can I go home?"

"That depends on how quickly you heal, young lady."

Nurse Stella popped her head inside. "She looks so much better today, doesn't she, Doctor?"

"Indeed. Keep her sedated as much as she needs for pain. I'll check in again later." He gazed at his notepad and strolled toward the hallway. "Good day, ladies."

When her breakfast tray came, the nurse fed her oatmeal. She opened her mouth like a babe in arms with each offered bite and envisioned how the nurse might react if she spit out her food like Emery did when he lost interest in his plate. Wouldn't he laugh to see his mommy now?

Oatmeal had never been a favorite of Teri's, but she had to admit the warmth felt good as the cereal slid down her throat. And the taste of real food...umm...how long had she been in that semiconscious state?

Daydreaming along with the book Teri chose passed the time between meals and intermittent hospital routine, but the ever-present ache in her heart reminded her how much she missed Clay and her children. When an elderly nurse walked into her room with a beautiful flower arrangement of yellow roses and baby's breath, her spirits soared. Stella set the vase on the chest of drawers opposite the bed where Teri could see them then read the card aloud. As beautiful as the arrangement was, Teri's heart sank when she heard they came from Smith Robinson instead of Clay.

Maybe her husband would surprise her instead. He could walk through the door any minute. The thought excited her. She wanted to be sure to look her best when Clay arrived, so she asked Stella for a mirror.

"I'll see if I can find one later. But if you have a comb in your purse, I can fetch that for you."

"I'd like that. Thank you."

Stella rummaged through Teri's bag. "Here we go." She handed the comb to Teri. "Dr. Morgan said you could sit by the window for a while. Would you like me to help you to the chair?"

"Um hm."

Once she settled Teri by the window, Stella shuffled toward the hallway and pulled the door closed behind her.

Teri tugged gently at the snarled hair protruding from under her bandages and worked until the strands felt smooth and glossy. She sat by the window and read until she nodded off.

A soft knock at the door awakened her, and she

gazed downward to be sure she looked presentable before she responded. Her heart beat faster as she prayed Clay had finally arrived. "Come in." Her meek, raspy voice wasn't what she wanted Clay to hear, but she could speak no clearer for wishing it so.

Mr. Robinson entered her room holding a box of candy. "Oh, Teri. It's so nice to see you're feeling better." He laid the candy on her side table and slipped off his coat. Pulling up the second chair, he sat and faced her. "How do you feel, honey?"

Stella interrupted in a brisk voice, "We are still a bit woozy, aren't we, dear?"

"Well, just take it easy and rest. Meg and I will take care of everything else."

Teri nodded and offered a faint smile. At least the tubes were gone, now, and her hair was combed...but what about the children? She wanted to see them...to assure them she was okay and would be home as soon as the doctors would allow. "How are Jenny and Emery?"

"This afternoon Meg took them to the park, and they were so excited. They both miss you... and they said to give you a kiss for them... and to hurry up and get better. Meg is taking them to and from kindergarten. They're such sweet kids, Teri, and so well behaved. You should be so proud. Now, Meg and I see what having children is like, I wish even more we had children of our own."

Again, Teri smiled. "Do you suppose they can come visit me?" At the thought, she sat up and straightened her posture.

Rob gazed at the nurse. Her pressed lips and a

quick shake of her head told him no.

"I think we should give you a few more days of rest. Maybe over the weekend, when both Meg and I can bring them."

Teri nodded. "Mr. Robinson, did the doctor tell you I'd be all right?"

"Why, yes. I believe he mentioned you were healing quite well."

"Then…" A sharp pain throbbed through her head and her hand flew to the source. She closed her eyes briefly until the ache subsided.

"Are you okay, dear?"

"Yes. Just a twinge of pain. The doctor said those pangs were a sign the injury was healing." A flash of Clay ran through her thoughts. Had she been thinking of only herself? If she'd be home soon, perhaps alerting her husband could wait. She knew he'd drop everything and come home, and she knew this trip was so important to his career. Dragging him home from such an important job was selfish. "On second thought, don't wire Clay and ask him to return. Please. This job is too important."

For a brief moment, Rob gave her an odd stare. "Oh…All right, Teri…I promise I won't cable Clay."

She relaxed into the chair. Her head still ached terribly, but she needed to think of her husband. Her hospital stay was just a blip on their future and their life together.

Stella motioned for Rob to leave.

He stood and tugged on his jacket lapel then shuffled his feet. "Meg will stop by tomorrow and bring you some things she gathered together." He turned and left the room in silence.

"Let's get you back to bed, hun." Stella lifted Teri's slight frame from the chair.

Draping an arm around the nurse's shoulder, Teri hobbled toward her bed, then slid under the cool white sheet. Her mind spun with thoughts of Clay and the children. But a stray thought occurred…was it her imagination, or did Mr. Robinson react oddly to her request to not wire her husband? Something about his reaction gave her pause, but she was so exhausted…and the notion was probably her imagination…like Scarlet O'Hara, she'd worry about that tomorrow.

Chapter Fifteen

T wo more days of storms took its toll on all three men. Suffering from exhaustion, Clay hooked an arm over the side of the vessel and clung to it as he dozed off and on—until his grip relaxed. When his hand splashed into water now raising above his waist, he awoke with a jerk, sending a shock of salty brine into his face. He gazed around to assess the situation. The last squall abated overnight, but the raft, already half-awash with seawater, tossed up and down over thick rollers from the receding storm. With each wave, a surge splashed over the edge sending the tiny dinghy deeper and deeper into the sea.

In a panic, Clay's gaze snapped toward Lou.

Face pale, he lay still...silent, his head bobbing with the rhythm of the sea, floating just above water.

Clay clambered across the raft and checked his pulse...a slow, weak, but steady beat. Thank God. He climbed behind Lou's shoulders and slid both hands under his arms then yanked his body, so it rested higher on the bulge of the dinghy.

Lou let out a wispy moan. In a morphine stupor, he slept through the storms, his shallow breathing barely lifting his chest.

A splash from behind caught Clay's attention, and he turned to see James lunging toward the radio.

Jim snatched the device from a pool and wiped off the water with his hand. Gazing around for a dry spot, he came to the same conclusion as Clay, "Everything on the boat is drenched." He vigilantly placed the radio on the driest spot he saw.

"How about the first aid kit?" Pinching the rations in his fingertips, Clay flipped the packages back and forth so the tiny pools of water would roll off. He offered some to Jim.

"Our medical supplies are about as waterproof as anything we have, but for safe-keeping, I tied the kit to the top of the pole last night." He took a cracker and bit the edge then chewed slowly.

"Good idea." Clay lowered his gaze to the ration box and chose a piece of chocolate.

Edging toward the canteen, Jim put it to his lips and took a drink. After a few sips, he lowered the tin, and his gaze locked on Clay's.

Narrowing his stare, Clay squinted. Despite gathering fresh water from the rain, they had no idea how long they'd be lost at sea. They needed to drink sparingly...especially considering Lou's injury. No telling when they'd spot land. If they ran out of water—a shiver down his arms stopped Clay from continuing the scenario.

Chin jutting forward, again, Jim held the canteen to his mouth and swallowed a few more gulps, his stare locked on Clay's.

If looks could kill, Jim would be six feet under. Clay forced a glare so intense he imagined it burning into Jim's eyes. "Don't push me, boy."

"Why not?" Jim spit on the edge of the raft. "It's fun to see how far you bend before you break, white boy. We'll see who comes out on top in the end."

Clay tossed him another scowl. "We have enough to do to keep afloat without your smartass games. Grab what you can to bail this water before we sink."

Jim's seething glower shot daggers. "Yes sur, massa sur." He frowned then turned and scuttled to the middle of the boat. Snatching the medical kit, he emptied the contents on a semi-dry spot then held up the empty tin toward Clay.

Again, Clay scowled. "It's my turn to crank." He grabbed the radio and started the tedious job then turned and peered over his shoulder. "Start bailing, James."

A cold hatred burned between them.

Jim sloshed his way to the end of the dinghy and began scooping water over the side.

A soft breeze cleared the sky as the storm edged its way to the Northeast. The crank grinding hummed in unison to the splash of water as James bailed, a duet broken only by Lou's occasional moans as he shifted positions.

When his arm strength gave out, Clay passed the radio to James and bailed the remaining water.

His head pounded and the heat only intensified the throbbing pain. He grabbed the canteen and took a swig.

Lou coughed then called to Clay, "Do I have to bail to earn a drink of water?"

Clay turned and gave him a smile. "It's about time you woke up." He scrabbled toward Lou then held the canteen to his lips.

Lou swallowed a few sips then pushed against the raft to pull himself upward, but the struggle was too much. He collapsed backward and let out a weary huff.

Concerned for his friend, Clay capped the canteen. "Here, let me help." He adjusted Lou's position then sat beside him. With no means to treat his wounds, Lou would continue to deteriorate. If they didn't find land soon—again, he halted and shook his head to dismiss the gloomy thought. Focusing on what ifs would only serve to drain his hope and that would accomplish nothing. He nudged Lou. "Can I get you something to eat? We don't have much, but it would do you good to nibble on a cracker or a small piece of chocolate."

Lou declined with a weak gesture.

Pressing his lips together, Clay shifted his gaze toward Jim. Purposely keeping an eye on the man, until if and when he proved himself trustworthy, Clay wondered how the black man was holding up. He'd made no qualms about letting Clay know he'd take what he wanted. Desperation did strange things to a man, and from what he'd seen of Jim so far, the man carried a heavy chip on his shoulder. Clay didn't trust him as far as he could throw him.

Wild animals killed to survive, caring nothing about their victims. Jim showed his disdain for white men at the airport, and the more time Clay spent around the man, the more he felt hatred burn between them. If push came to shove, would he share the limited food and water? Clay thought not, and his stare deepened with mistrust.

Lips visibly dry and cracking, Jim churned the radio, staring blankly into the monotonous rhythmic swells ever reaching for the horizon. Streams of sweat trickled from his brow, and his black skin glistened as the sun beat down and reflected off the perspiration. He cranked in a rhythmic cadence, as if humming a beat within his mind. Perhaps that made the job more tolerable.

Clay gazed along the horizon, searching for some sign of land. He recalled the pilot had mentioned the Phoenix Islands right before the plane entered the band of storm clouds. From what he remembered when he studied the flight's route, that would place them somewhere between the Phoenix Islands and American Samoa...the Archipelago. Dozens of islands peppered the area. With any luck, the tiny raft would drift toward civilization. But a deserted island would suffice, as long as it had fresh water and edible vegetation.

Eyes burning from the glare, Clay squinted. In the distance, he noticed a patch of darkening clouds. *Dear God, please, not another storm.* Perhaps the formation was a low-lying fog...ghostly gray on the horizon. He craned his neck as if doing so would strengthen his vision. Could the haze be...his pulse kicked up a beat. Was he seeing the image of...land? Speaking softly to avoid disturbing Lou, he stumbled toward Jim, pointing his finger. "What do you see on the horizon out there?"

Shielding his eyes from the sun, he glared. "Water."

The raft bobbed up and down on the waves, and Clay steadied his stance by grabbing Jim's shoulder. "Look farther, where the ocean meets the horizon."

Jim lowered his gaze to his shoulder and Clay's clenched hand pressing hard, then he tossed a frown toward Clay.

Immediately, Clay released his grasp. "Sorry."

Again, Jim held a hand above his eyes and peered at the horizon. "Too far away to tell for sure. Like the desert sand, seawater can fool a man's mind into believing something is there when it's not...like a mirage."

Clay pinched his brows together. Caught off guard, he was taken aback at Jim's intellectual reply. "I wasn't sure whether my eyes were playing tricks or not. Guess we'll find out soon enough. The current has been pushing us in that direction for a while now.

"Might be an island, though. We could get there faster if we row." Jim reached for a paddle.

This time intentionally, Clay grasped Jim's arm. "Wait. The Phoenix Islands are known for their treacherous coral reefs. Maybe we should save our energy until we get a bit closer. If that shadow is an island, we might need all our energy to row ashore. The current around those reefs could force us around the island and out to sea or thrust us over the jagged rocks."

Jim nodded. "That's a good point."

"I'm about cooked from this heat. What do you say we both crawl under the canopy? We can watch our approach from there then take action when we get closer. Clay wiped the sweat from his brow then scuttled under the tarp toward Lou.

Jim hesitated then ducked under the shelter. "Any change in Lou's condition?"

"No. But at least he's resting more peacefully."

Though the canvas blocked the sun, it also blocked any breeze that might cool the men from the sweltering heat. It was hot as hell, but better than blistering from the sun reflecting off the ocean.

Restlessly, the men huddled beneath the canvas, taking turns to stand and stretch, and peer in the distance at the shadow on the horizon.

His patience wearing thin, Clay could sit no longer. He crawled into the open air and stood spread-eagle to keep his balance. Gazing across bobbing waves, he wondered how men spent months on schooners in the olden days just to cross the great oceans. How spoiled he was with modern technology, electric refrigerators and fans, automobiles, and planes. What he would do right now for a simple ice cube.

He squinted and stared at the shadow stretching along the horizon. Was he wishful thinking, or could he distinguish a distinct knob jutting toward the sky...a shadow like that could only be one thing...the crest of a long-extinct volcano—a volcano that gave birth to most of the Pacific Islands? With a long sigh of relief, he lowered to his hands and knees, then scrambled back to Jim and Lou.

As Clay approached, Jim sat forward and stared, his stance rigid and jaw clenched.

Grinning, Clay nodded. "It's an island, Jim." Relief flooded his extremities. "With any luck, we should make land before dark."

A smile spread wide across Jim's ebony face, and he crawled toward the open air to see for himself. Standing with splayed legs, he let out a long deep chuckle. Despite his dry cracked lips, he flopped onto the raft in the blistering sunshine and stretched full-length, propping his head against the side so he could watch as the shadow grew.

Clay shook his head, noting the black man's reaction so similar to his own.

"I hope your grin isn't due to a private joke. I could use some good cheer."

Clay turned to face Lou. "Land, Lou. We can see an island in the distance, and we should be there just in time for dinner."

Lou pushed against the dinghy to sit higher, then cringed and resigned to stay put. "Make my steak rare, son."

"Here, let me help you." Clay leaned close and slid an arm under Lou then tugged. "That's better. I wish I could do something more to ease your discomfort. Is the morphine relieving at least some of the pain?"

"For a while." Voice labored, Lou drew in a few shallow breaths. "I'm sure I'll feel better once we're on dry land."

Assessing his friend's condition as best he

could, Clay decided Lou appeared a bit more relaxed and hoped that meant he was improving.

Jim watched their interaction then reached into his pocket. Pulling out a harmonica, he tapped it against his palm several times before cupping his fingers around the instrument and pressing it to his lips.

His music encircled the tiny raft, relaxing the crew for the first time since the crash.

Lou and Clay sat back and listened.

Jim definitely had talent. Clay couldn't recall if he'd heard the tune before, but the blues melody haunted him as he searched his memory. He closed his eyes, thankful for the diversion. Without Jim's soothing music, Clay would be monitoring their approach every few seconds as the island slowly grew into focus.

After playing several tunes, some rollicking and waggish, Jim paused then called out to Clay. "How about a drink of water to celebrate? My lips are too dry to play this mouth organ much longer."

Clay reached for the canteen then tossed it to Jim, who eagerly caught the vessel.

Pressing the can to his lips, he gulped down several swigs, then took in a long breath. He stood then scuttled toward Lou and offered him a drink.

Lou accepted the proffer and gave Jim a cursory nod. He took a few drinks before passing the canteen to Clay.

Returning to his harmonica, Jim situated himself then continued his serenade.

The water was cool and refreshing. Clay took several swallows before setting the container aside.

As the island drew closer, Clay crawled out from under the canopy to check the distance, wind, and current. He searched the shoreline for any sign of inhabitants, be they animal or human, but he saw no movement. The island appeared to be about two miles long, not including coral reefs jutting out to the south. "What do you think the chances are of finding anyone on that island?"

Jim raised his gaze toward Clay. "I haven't seen a soul. But I did see a structure off to the left. It looks like a shack of some sort...back in that grove of palms." He pointed toward the hut.

Staring at the cove, Clay became increasingly aware of the rushing current. He gazed across the ocean's surface for several long moments. The raft was changing course. No longer was the small dinghy approaching the beach. Instead, the current shifted the vessel toward the coral reef jutting out some four or five hundred yards from the coast in a scythe-like semi-circle. The counter current would force them around the southern edge of the island then out to sea. Clay sprang into action, snatching two paddles. "This is the end of the free ride, Jim. From now on, we work." He tossed an oar to Jim then started rowing.

Jim slipped off his shoes and eased his body over the edge of the dinghy into the deep-blue water. Placing his hands at the stern, he commenced a steady flutter-kick, pushing the vessel forward.

Clay stared at the shift in the boat's direction. *I'll be damned.* He yelled toward Jim, "Move over to the other corner...to compensate for the thrust of the paddle."

Jim nodded and slid his palms to the opposite side.

They worked together, fighting the current as the vessel drifted past the southern edge of the island. When they finally broke free from the current, the boat shifted...and headed straight into the jagged coral. The tumult of breakers let out a deafening, ceaseless roar and shot a torrential spray upward until gravity forced the gushing flow downward against the jagged rocks.

Clay spotted a break in the reef and shouted over the thunder of crashing breakers. "One scrape of that coral and this raft will explode like a pin in a toy balloon. Watch yourself, Jim. Keep close to the surface."

Jim acknowledged the warning with a cursory nod.

Again, Clay bellowed. "I doubt sharks swim in this torrent...but if they do and that coral cuts you to the point of drawing blood...we are all dead."

Jim glanced around the surface then hollered. "We have no choice but to cross the coral. You ready?"

"Let's go. Take it easy until we get a feel for the current's thrust." As they approached the break in the coral, a large wave rolled beneath the surface and lifted them forward, but when the swell ebbed, Clay gasped as the dip revealed a tree-like shard of coral projecting upward right in their path. He dove into the water. Paddling feverishly, he shouted over his shoulder, "Left, Jim. Push hard to the left."

Letting off for a minute, as he turned the front

of the raft toward the opening, he could feel the boat slow as Jim heaved. Again, a wave plunged them toward the jagged projection. Clay hoisted himself over the edge of the lifeboat and grabbed the oar. Clinging for his life onto the slippery rubber, he shoved the paddle toward the coral, hitting a smaller protruding limb. With a loud snap, the paddle gave way. The sudden release threw him off balance and hurled him into the deadly swirling water.

Chapter Sixteen

C linging with one hand onto the oar, Clay shoved the paddle between him and the coral, scrambling to stay free of the razor-like edges. When the oar made contact, the impact thrust him upward like a rag doll and shot him forward into a huge breaker. He stiffened and rose to the surface, searching madly for the raft. Spying the lifeboat about a hundred yards away and drifting toward him, he swam forward. The waves pushing toward the shore assisted his trek.

Jim leaned over the side and hoisted Clay aboard.

Once inside, he could see what he assumed was a clean break in the reef was, in reality, a shallow saddle no more than a few feet deep at best. He lunged forward and grabbed the mast holding the canopy, letting the canvas flutter across Lou. Turning, he shouted to Jim, "Grab the other corner and get over to the far side."

Lunging forward, Jim ripped the canopy

upward as a new wave surged.

Seeing the tiny boat leaning into another coral branch protruding from the reef, Clay jabbed at the spikes.

Jim immediately followed suit.

Together, they stabbed at the barbs, barely managing to keep the raft free from the death trap. Another breaker threatened...but catching a jagged cliff below created a riptide motion that twisted the raft's trajectory, lifting the tiny boat and pushing it gently toward the shore.

Panting and soaked to the skin, both men collapsed onto the canvas, exhausted from their exertion. They gasped for breath as the tiny raft floated into a quiet lagoon.

"Dear God. What the hell happened?" Lou tugged at the corner of the canvas and groaned, then peeked under the edge. "Can one of you..." He kicked at the tarp, wincing with each exertion. "Please...get this thing off of me?"

Clay cast a weary gaze at Jim before moving a muscle. "I'll get it, buddy." He gulped in a lungful of air then yanked the edge of the canopy and heaved it aside.

Lou rose carefully onto one arm until he could peer over the edge of the lifeboat. The ocean sparkled as if dotted with diamonds. The lagoon, so crystal clear and blue, he could see details in the coral formations. A small parrot fish swam lazily in and out of the swaying fronds. A turtle made a slow arc then inquisitively nosed its head out of the water for a moment before ducking once again and continuing on its way.

Lou arched higher and inspected the shoreline. A white sandy beach, gleaming as the sunlight reflected off crystalline sparkles, blanketed the approach to a palm grove with a dense jungle beyond. A soft breeze swayed the palm leaves. Set under the grove, a small shack stood desolate and lonely. Seagulls circled endlessly overhead, occasionally darting into the water in search of a meal. Lou smiled and slumped, gently laying his head against the bulge in the raft. He'd hovered under the canopy unable to help, while Clay and Jim together had fought the battle to save their lives. He sighed, abhorring the agonizing feeling of helplessness.

Having lost the paddle at sea, Clay and Jim slipped into the sea and pushed the raft, kicking behind until the dinghy reached shallow water. Once they could stand on the bottom, they slogged toward the shore, assisted by the current pushing small waves beneath the tiny craft. Then, with a final burst of energy, they heaved the raft onto the beach, away from the lapping waves.

Clay took off his shirt and shoes and drew in several long breaths before strolling toward the shack. After peering inside the gloomy hut for a moment or two, he turned and strolled back to Lou and Jim.

Without asking, Lou knew the hut was deserted. "Looks like that place is up for rent. What do you say, boys? Shall we lease it for a while?"

"Sounds like a good plan." Jim snatched the canvas and dragged it under the palm grove then straightened the edges across the sand near the shack. After inspecting his work, he raised his gaze and called out, "This looks like a nice spot to stretch out. What do you think, Lou?" Returning to the raft, he nudged Clay and hitched his head. "What do you say we help this man onto dry land?"

Carefully, Clay and Jim lifted Lou and carried him toward the shack.

"What's your pleasure, Lou, inside or outside?" Clay asked.

He scanned the beach. "The tarp is fine. Jim chose the perfect spot under the shade of those palms."

Carefully, the two men lowered him to the canvas.

"Excellent room service, gentlemen. Much appreciated." Lou felt his energy wane and a wave of nausea rolled through his stomach. He swallowed to ease the sensation. "I think I might need a day or two on dry land to stabilize my sea legs."

Clay stood and stretched. "With any luck, we'll find civilization as we move inland, but I have my doubts. This is a small island, and if people live here, they'd likely settle close to shore."

"That deserted shack gives me an eerie feeling this island is uninhabited." Jim turned toward the raft. "I reckon we should grab the gear then start a fire. The weather is warm, but a fire should scare off any wild animals wandering the jungle."

Lou nodded. "I wish I could give you two a hand."

"Don't you worry. After what we've been through, I don't think anything could arise that Clay and I can't handle." Jim shifted his gaze to Clay. "Why don't you check on his wound? I'll fetch the supplies."

"Good idea. Grab the medical kit first. Now that we're on dry land, we can get a better look at Lou's chest and back."

Lou watched Jim stroll toward the raft then turned his focus to his injuries. He leaned forward so Clay could help him take off his shirt then twisted to inspect his side, but the motion shot a stabbing pain through his ribs. He winced and bit the inside of his lip to keep from groaning.

Clay lifted his hands and drew back. "Did I hurt you?"

"Nah, I tried to turn, but my chest didn't cooperate." He peered at Clay. The man looked worried. Lou was worried, too. He hoped once he got on dry land, he'd feel a marked improvement, but after the coral reef incident, his pain intensified. He knew his ribs were broken. The violent sea tossing him to-and-fro for days on end didn't help. What he needed most was sleep. *Keep a cool head, Lou…and stoic attitude. You'll get through this.* Now that Bobbie was in his life, he had a lot to look forward to. He was finally off that wretched raft and could take it easy and let his broken ribs heal.

When Jim returned with the gear, he handed Clay the medical kit, then set the rest of the supplies inside the hut. "The clear weather means rescue teams can finally search for survivors, don't you think? Even if this island is deserted, someone is bound to find us." He handed Lou the medical kit.

Raising a brow, Clay flattened his lips. "Assuming they don't find the wreckage and presume all the passengers and crew perished in the crash."

"Don't fill your head with negative thoughts." Jim knelt next to Lou then sat back onto his calves. "We need to gather wood and make a fire…and it wouldn't hurt to dig a big SOS into the damp sand. Maybe someone flying overhead will see the message in the sand or the smoke and send help."

"Great idea, Jim. I wonder how far that storm carried us from the crash site." Lou shifted his gaze between the two other men."

"I'll scrape the SOS into the sand then look for kindling." Jim stood. "If we gather enough wood to keep a fire burning constantly, I'm sure someone will find us."

"Hopefully you're right." Clay tossed him a glance. "The quicker Mr. Rosson receives professional medical care, the happier I'll be."

Jim halted mid-step. He turned and shot Clay a look of disdain. After a long moment of silence, he spoke. "Back to Mr. is it?"

Lou saw the rage rise on Jim's face, and he shook his head then watched Clay's reaction.

Clearly oblivious to the exchange, Clay spoke without looking up. "Early tomorrow morning, I'll investigate the island. We have enough food here to take care of us for the night, but if this island is uninhabited, we will need more water and food. If I find civilization on the other side of the island, I'll bring back help."

Casting a seething glare, Jim snatched a handful of rations and tramped toward the beach.

Clay stood and frowned, staring after him. "Now what the devil prompted that?"

Jim traipsed toward the raft. With the heal of his foot, he dug a huge SOS into the sand then proceeded down the beach with stiff steps and a heavy tread.

The puzzled expression splashed over Clay's face needed no explanation.

"You don't even know what you said, do you, son?" Lou pressed his lips together.

"Who me?" Clay glanced around then settled his gaze on Lou. "What are you talking about? Did I say something wrong?"

Lou pushed his chest upward and leaned back, his palms supporting his trunk. "You and Jim worked together on that raft night and day. He saved us more than once, so why did you say, *The quicker we get Mr. Rosson real medical care, the happier you'd be*? That snide comment instantly dropped his status ten feet beneath you."

He waved a hand. "Aw, come on, Lou. We worked together and were safe. Can't we leave it at that? Why should I grovel to the boy because I inadvertently hurt his feelings? I didn't demean him intentionally."

Lou shook his head. "No. You don't have to grovel." He leaned onto his elbows. "But tell me, son…why doesn't Jim deserve the same respect as you give me? I didn't lift a finger to help us get to this island. And you haven't known me much longer."

133

Turning toward the beach and ocean beyond, Clay raked a hand through his hair and glared at Jim in silence.

Disgusted he'd let Clay's comment get to him so easily, Jim huffed. After all these years, he should have hardened to the white men's attitudes. But like a child lashing out at everything and everyone, every time he thought someone shot him down, he reacted instead of responded.

He kicked a piece of driftwood in his path then jerked away his foot in pain. The branch, half buried under the sand, didn't budge with his blow. After brushing aside the sand, he sat on the log and rubbed his foot then gazed across the blue-green sea. For a little while, he'd almost forgotten he was a second-class citizen. Now that they were safely ashore, the relationship volleyed back to black versus white. He grimaced at the painful reality. *Always, mister.* He grabbed a handful of sand and scoured the backs of his hands. Don't white folks ever see beyond the color of his skin? No matter what he contributed...regardless of his education...his skill, the black stain remained. Taking his fist, he beat the ground while a single tear escaped and rolled down his cheek.

When Jim finally returned to the shack, the sun had dipped below the horizon. Clay had been busy. He gathered a few pieces of wood, lit a small fire...found some spindly bananas and a couple of coconuts and was busy breaking one with a heavy rock.

Jim approached quietly and emptied his arms of the driftwood load he had gathered along the beach.

Clay offered a curt nod and continued his task.

Lou sat against the palms where they perched him earlier. He watched Jim pick up a few pieces of wood and place them on the fire. "A hundred men might make an encampment, but it takes a woman to make a home. Come on, Jim, sit and join us in our meager attempt."

Jim gazed at Lou and flashed him a grin.

"Here, catch." Clay called out.

Spinning a stare, Jim saw a coconut flying toward his face. He dodged the bullet, allowing the coconut to fall to the ground behind him. He shot a defiant gaze toward Clay before turning his attention to Lou. Strolling to his side, he knelt on one knee. "Is there anything I can do to make you more comfortable...*Mr. Rosson*?"

Lou stared, his jaw set. "Yes. Drop the Mr. Rosson. I don't know your last name, Jim, but after all we've been through, I don't believe last names matter much. Don't you agree?"

Jim sat back onto his calves, picked up a random rock then methodically hit it against the eye of a coconut. Speaking low, he directed his conversation toward Lou. "Rucker." He lifted his gaze to meet Lou's. "My last name is Rucker." He lifted the coconut and slammed it onto the rock, immediately breaking the hard shell then turned to face Lou. "I swore I'd never use that name again."

Chapter Seventeen

As Jim spoke, evening shadows lengthened and dusk dimmed over the small lagoon. Clay broke some crackers and added them to the bananas and coconut milk then set them beside the fire. After placing a portion in front of Lou, he sat and listened.

Jim gazed at the blazing fire spiraling embers into the darkening sky, and he noticed how the white banyan trees stood out against the deep velvet night. "Shall I tell you the story of old black Joe, Mr. Clayton? A poor, ignorant, black man who fell in love with a white woman? You should keep your women safe, Mr. Clayton, away from dangerous, dirty black men like me." He spit out with a bitter twang. "On second thought, Mr. Clayton...I think I'll tell you the story of a young black boy and how he learnt to hate so well his momma couldn't recognize him."

Jim lowered his head between his hands and spoke, his anger spent. "His father was what you folks would call 'a good Negro.' He had little education, but what need did a field boy have for education? He married and moved north, hoping to distance themselves from the poverty they both had known all their lives. He heard up north held opportunities. He found a job as a night janitor in a small factory and, during the day, he worked his hide off as a gardener. He was black as night, but what a green thumb he had. He could make anything grow."

"That black man's wife took in ironing and, between them, they managed to save enough money to buy a small house at the edge of town where the well-to-do blacks lived. Before long, he had his little yard blooming with flowers from leftover seeds he used in his day jobs. Mind you, those seeds were gifts from the white folks he worked for, not stolen without their knowledge." Jim reached for a stick by the stack of firewood then stoked the logs until the blaze brightened the area around the campfire.

"My momma and daddy never wanted children, Mr. Clayton. They knew how much misery a black child was given as a birthright. When I look at the past, I mostly remember my mother crying. Oh, I remember the good times too, but mostly the tears." He pushed from the fiery glow then leaned on his elbows and crossed his legs.

"I recall my first day in school. I didn't go to a segregated school, Mr. Clayton. Oh, no. The Northerners had integration. Two-hundred kids went to my school, and maybe seven or eight of our kind scattered through the grades. I learned my place quickly." The flickering flames cast shadows that danced across his arms and made his sweaty skin glisten. Memories swirling, he continued his story.

"Recess was a good teacher, school parties, Parent's Day...yes, I quickly learnt the kind of friendship the coloreds had in a school of white folks. The coach wanted me on the football team, but even then, I had to be careful. I couldn't be too good, or I'd show up a white boy. Lord knows I couldn't afford to do that...but if I pretended to be worse than those white boys, I'd be benched...or kicked off the team. So, I learnt to balance on a double-edged sword."

The fire crackled as glowing embers floated upward into the night sky. Jim leaned forward again and rested his elbows on his knees as the swirling memories caused his stomach to tighten.

"As I grew older, the school held dances in the gym. Sure, I could go and watch on the sidelines. But even then, I had to be careful. A single glance was all it took. A white boy thought he saw me staring at a white girl...the beating left scars no man should endure—but still, I felt lucky. I loved to read about the wondrous places I would visit one day, and the world of dreams I'd hold in my hands if I worked hard at my studies." He carved off a piece of coconut and popped it into his mouth. After swallowing the bite, he continued.

"My parents were strict. Momma wouldn't allow me to run around with the riffraff our side of town produced, and society forbade me to associate with my classmates. So, I studied...alone. All the

139

time, I studied. I could compete with my mind and my knowledge. My grades were damn good, and I graduated high school in the upper ten percent of the class. I graduated with honors, in spite of my esteemed Northern classmates and some bitter teachers who didn't want a black boy to excel. I succeeded...and I thought I had the world in my pocket." He picked up the canteen and took a swig, hoping the water would wash down the bile seeping into his throat. It didn't. He offered the jug to Lou.

Accepting the proffer, Lou took a drink then lowered the canteen.

Jim shook his head. "For me, college boards were a snap. I applied to a couple of different colleges. Filled out the forms and return them. I won't go into how that turned out...suffice to say I was finally accepted—I'll give that to the North, I was accepted and attended a good college. The summer before my first year, I worked like a dog waiting tables...mowing lawns for white folks...anything to make money. Momma and Daddy scrimped and saved, too, and I finally had enough to pay my tuition."

"The school assigned me a single room in the dormitory. Funny, I was the only freshman with that distinction. Still, I thought I earned my way— until the college kids treated me the same as the high schoolers...I'd seen that movie before, though, and I was wiser. This time I kept to myself and avoided social embarrassment." He lifted his gaze and peered at the starlit sky.

"Every free minute I had, I worked odd jobs to make more money. I cleaned the furnace room, waited on tables, scrubbed stoves, and most times I'd fall into bed too tired to sleep...for three summers I worked every waking minute. And in the winter, I went to school and studied.

"When my third year started, I hit the books even harder and, by the end of the second quarter, I was at the top of my junior class. Next to me in that prestigious line was a boy who seemed to have everything he wanted...a good family and popular as hell." He lowered his gaze and turned to Lou. "You know the kind."

Lou nodded. "That I do, son...that I do."

"Well, sir...before long, the two of us competed in a kind of race to see which of us earned better grades. One day, when third-quarter exams were coming up, I noticed that fella's attitude took a sudden change. Out of nowhere, the kid acted like he didn't care about the competition and shrugged off studying."

"I didn't have time to deal with his problems. I worked in the cafeteria and between classes helped out in reproductions. I kept my schedule timed to the minute. My afternoon classes started at two o'clock, so I left the cafeteria at quarter-to-two then raced to my room to pick up my books for my afternoon classes.

"The day before the big exam, I had just switched out my books and closed my dormitory door, when that kid...he approached me and asked if he could borrow a textbook. Said he misplaced his. I said sure and let him into my room. He promised he'd close the door behind him when he left. I can still remember the relief I felt at his

141

change in attitude."

The fire, now settling, crackled and threw sparks into the night sky. The remaining kindling fell against the flickering embers. Clay reached over and grabbed some logs then quietly placed them on the fire.

Jim gazed at the flames as they licked around the logs then reached upward into the darkness. The sound of the surf breaking on the shoals and the nocturnal animals rustling through the forest inside the belly of the island made the fire even more hypnotic. The orange flames burned, reaching higher and higher, warming the front of Jim's body against the cool dampness of the evening. Mesmerized by the glow, he relived that fateful day.

"I think I'm going to hit the hay. Thanks for the bedtime story, Jim." Clay stood then leaned over Lou. "Can I get you anything before I turn in?"

"No, but I'd like to hear the rest of Jim's story, if he doesn't mind."

Jim nodded.

"Then I'll see you two in the morning." Clay turned and strolled into the shack then closed the door behind him.

"Go on, Jim."

Again, Jim stoked the fire then edged closer to Lou. "The next morning, I was in class ready for the exam. I knew the test would be easy. I'd studied and kept notes all year and I knew the material backwards and forwards. The monitors passed out the sheets, and I read the first question."

"The room quieted. All I could hear was

pencils scratching against paper. Occasionally, I heard the rasp of erasers as someone scrubbed out an answer they didn't like. I had no trouble with the questions. Finishing the paper well within the allotted hour, I gathered my books, walked to the front, and put my paper on the professor's desk. I turned to leave the room, and the professor followed me into the hall. He took hold of my upper arm to stop me then quietly closed the classroom door."

"The professor gazed at the floor like he didn't want to look me in the eye. He said he overheard talk I stole copies of my final exam from the reproduction room. Then he lifted his gaze to meet mine and said, 'Son, I know your grades are topnotch, but I have no choice but to check into the accusation.'"

"My knees went weak. I felt like somebody punched me in the stomach."

"Did you deny the charge?" Lou asked with honest concern.

"I protested my innocence and naturally agreed to have my room searched, knowing full well they'd find no proof of something I didn't do..." Jim paused and watched Lou's reaction.

Closing his eyes, he shook his head.

"You guessed the rest of my story, right? I never had a chance." He stood and kicked at some lingering embers.

"Of course, they found the papers in my room. But who would believe my side of the story over the boys who claimed I cheated? Who would suspect someone of impeccable background planted the papers in my room? It was far easier to drum me out of the school. From that day on, no reputable school would accept my application." He shot a gaze toward the shack door, wishing Clay stayed to hear the rest of his story.

"Black is a miraculous color. It's surprising how the pigment can magically make opportunity disappear." He turned to face Lou. "My momma died that winter, and my dad might as well have joined her. He fell into the bottle, boozing away everything he once held dear."

"And you?" Lou raised a brow.

"Me...ha, ha. I took off, hopped freight trains across the country...anything I could do to lose myself...but I couldn't go far enough to forget. I hated the world...and the world made it damn easy to oblige."

Lou dropped his gaze to the ground.

Jim went silent as the night. Even the calls of nocturnal animals hushed in the stillness, and the quiet shrouded him like a sodden blanket.

Lou raised his gaze and peered directly into Jim's eyes. "Often when a man unburdens his soul, he comes to hate those to whom he divulged the truth. I should not like to think of that happening to you and me, Jim. It's easy for me to sympathize, but difficult to offer any acceptable solutions." Lou attempted to pull himself into a sitting position, but he fell backward against the palm tree.

Jim jumped to his aid and lifted him to a more comfortable position.

Lou nodded a thank you. "Jim...society isn't perfect in anyone's eyes. But we must all remember the only effective way to change society is to work together with every thought, every skin color, every faith, and creed. It's only when we work together will we re-mold society into what we believe it can be. To attack with vengeance is to destroy the possibility of creating a better world...and the destruction will bring down all individuals as the dream collapses. If you hear a word I say tonight...hear this...if you're not part of the answer...you're part of the problem."

Jim listened to Lou as he spoke of the unperfect world and of hope for a future where all men and women would live harmoniously together. When Lou tired, he leaned back against the palm tree and closed his eyes.

Jim stood and eased his friend off the tree to a more comfortable position on the tarp. Stretching out and lost in his own thoughts, Jim mindlessly picked up a knarred piece of driftwood and poked at the fire until the blaze rekindled. The world would have to do a whole lot of changing to approach Lou's harmonious vision.

Casi McLean

Chapter Eighteen

Lou laid awake long after his companions had fallen asleep. He held his pain at bay before the others turned in, but his head throbbed, and his body ached so badly he could hardly tell where the pain began. He clenched his teeth. With the morphine dwindling, he wondered how much longer he could manage. Oddly enough, the medicine didn't really ease his pain. But when he took a pill, he felt detached from the agony as if watching himself suffer from the outside looking in.

Thoughts reeling over the conversation with Jim, Lou wished for more clarity. The points he wanted Jim to understand were poorly stated. In his drug-induced condition, the right words simply didn't surface. His mind spun, and the pain caused him to break into a cold sweat. The night ebbed onward as he tossed and turned aching and awake, wishing the dawn would break and at least distract him from the chasm pulling him downward and away from what he wanted most...Bobbie.

Clay lay beside the hut's only window and stared at the starry sky until the two men outside quieted. He closed his eyes and thought about Jim's story and what Lou had said by the fireside that night. Surely, Jim realized his schoolboy treatment was not personally directed, but rather an indication of the dissidence of others in his race. What irked Clay was Jim's behavior at the airport. The chip on that boy's shoulder needed adjustment. Clay had never thought of himself as a prejudiced man, but Jim brought out the worst in people with his everyone-owes-me attitude.

Staring through the window at flickering shadows cast by the fire's glow, Clay wondered when this nightmare would end. How many days had passed since he left Teri? He could only imagine how she took the news of the crash. She must be out of her mind with worry...or grief. Dear God, when will someone find them so they could go home?

The next morning, Clay woke early. He quietly replenished the firewood and was pleased to see Lou resting. Recalling his promise to walk around the island, he pulled together a few supplies, wrote a note to Lou in the hard sand then began his hike along the beach. Despite the early hour, the sunshine warmed his back.

Sand crabs scurried across his path, busily searching for their morning meal. He paced forward for what had to be at least an hour, probing beyond the wooded area for signs of habitation. The only sounds he heard were birds chirping and small animals rustling through the underbrush in the jungle area of the island.

The forest, thick with coconut palms, elephant ears, and a menagerie of plants, took on the appearance of vines as they twisted and snaked their way upward to reach the sun. As the beach curved around the island, the shore thrust a finger into the sea. Clay dug his toes into the sand and paused for a moment to gaze seaward, hoping against hope he'd see the shiny glint of an airplane in the distance or a ship adrift on the sea. Instead, only the obscene emptiness of the sky met his gaze. The touch of coarse salt air swept across his face, and he breathed in deeply before turning to continue his hike. As he plodded around the island, he thought about what they knew so far.

The shack where they camped was previously use by fisherman who must have visited the island periodically. Would they return soon? Nothing here would lure fishermen other than the peace and quiet of the sea-swept beach. Water, sand, palms, and his own footprints in the sand were all Clay saw. When he approached the crook of the island, the finger of the coral reef surrounding the lagoon loomed in the distance, reflecting the sunlight like a silver disk. This view of the island would be forever impressed upon his mind.

Mango trees crowded the shoreline. He traipsed forward and picked a few. What other vegetation grew close by? The wide array would provide an endless trove to keep the castaways fed and strong for months to come—if need be. Today, mangoes were on the menu. Placing the fruit carefully in a pile to one side, he heard the distinctive sound of water cascading over rocks.

He turned inland and trudged through the jungle in search of fresh water. As a reward for finding the falls, he stood in the spray and washed the sea salt from his arms and legs, considering what he and Jim might use to carry some water back to camp. When he returned to the beach, he gazed across the waves toward the reef, then kicked off his shoes and pants and laid them on a gray coral hump cast upon the beach by some ancient storm.

Dressed only in his boxer shorts and an undershirt to protect his torso from the blistering sun, he waded into the water, then swam toward the coral to check for oysters or turtles to supplement their breakfast. Nearing the mound, he could see oysters inside the crevices scattered beneath the bar on the ocean side.

Returning to the shore, he hunted until he found a sharp conch shell to pry them loose, then turned and ran into the water, cutting it with a long clean dive. Dodging the waves, he dove again, then swam toward the reef. A cleansing exhilaration rushed over him as he swam through the warm, clear water, thoughts spinning to a happier time in his youth.

Growing up on the banks of the Savannah

River, Clay learned to swim at an early age. Despite parental warnings, he and his friends went swimming whenever they could. Fighting the swift current in the middle of the Savannah became second nature.

With a powerful stroke, he whooshed through the sparkling water toward the coral shelf. When he surfaced, he spit out saltwater, then stood on the formation and shook the water from his hair. Spotting more oysters, he edged across the reef and positioned himself to best harvest his crop. While he was underwater, life slowed as if time itself moved at half speed. Hands clenched tightly against the shell, he chipped it from the hard, clean service where the oyster nested. Repeating the process over and over, he surfaced only to ease the torture of his breathless lungs.

After gathering roughly a dozen oysters, he took off his undershirt and tucked the shells into a makeshift pouch then tied it around his waist. At the edge of the shelf, he slid into deeper water, then flutter-kicked toward the shore. The persistent gentle tug of the waves threatened his stash, so he turned onto his back and floated to tighten the knot. After retrieving his pants and shoes, he added the mangoes to the pouch and headed back to camp.

As he approached the shack, Clay saw Jim sleeping flat on his back beneath the cluster of palms, an arm flung over his eyes to ward off the daylight.

Lou tossed quietly in a restless doze.

When Clay knelt to feel Lou's forehead, his foot bumped against a coconut stack.

Jim snapped awake and frowned at Clay. He pulled himself upward to sit, cold fire dancing in his gaze.

Returning the gesture, Clay shook his head. "This isn't Oahu Beach, Mr. Rucker. In case you haven't noticed, the motel is closed for the season. We have to fend for ourselves." He paused, waiting for a reaction that didn't come. "For one who is so sensitive to equal rights, may I point out equality is a two-way street? I found breakfast. You prepare the meal." Clay opened his undershirt pouch and let the load of oysters and mangoes tumble next to Jim.

Chapter Nineteen

J im snarled. "Okay, whitey, you want a fight? Let's end this right here…right now." From a crouch, he lunged forward with Clay in his crosshairs, tackling him just below the hips.

Clay turned his face and, in doing so, relinquished to the full impact of Jim's body. The force shoved him backward onto hard-packed sand. Jim's assault took him down, but snapping to his feet in a fluid ricochet, he responded, lunging forward with animal-like vengeance burning in his eyes.

The battle began.

Clay's right shoulder twisted as he brought his left elbow back, jabbing a vicious punch squarely into Jim's face.

Thrust backward with the force, Jim rebounded. Clawing Clay's leg to catch him off balance, he delivered a wild haymaker squarely into his face.

Clay ducked…the blow only grazed his left ear.

It might have stung, but it did little damage.

Lopsided from a near miss, Jim stumbled forward then spun to straighten his stance. He glared, his gaze targeting his nemesis like switchblades on a mark.

Shifting his feet slightly, Clay took Jim's next punch head on, but returned a jab that hit Jim in the forehead.

Stunned, Jim drew back to aim his reply but was blindsided when Clay slung a southpaw with a short jolting left then followed up with a right jab.

The contact slammed Jim as if he hit a brick wall. Anger seething, he launched forward and rammed his shoulder with a full-force jab into Clay's stomach. The man had to be aching from the force of Jim's blows.

But Clay's fist thrust forward.

Jim's weight and size gave him a clear advantage. He shoved his head upward, striking Clay on the tip of his chin.

Clay plowed forward into the brutal brawl.

Their savage attack whirled a sandstorm around their wildly swinging fisticuffs. Fist for fist and blow for blow, they tore into each other, neither able to deliver an ultimate knockout.

Finally, one hand free, Jim struck Clay with a wicked cut across his face, followed by a back-handed slap. His ring cut open Clay's lip, slicing a half-inch gouge that oozed a stream of blood down his chin and splattered scarlet droplets across the stark white sand.

Clay's wild fury stopped cold. Both arms flew in front of his face to ward off another punch.

Jim reared back and swung hard, taking advantage of his opponent's pause with a pummeling attack.

Clay raised his left elbow then yanked Jim's wrist with his right hand and twisted it over his head.

Jim whipped down with a staggering thrust, but Clay used Jim's momentum to roll him onto his side.

Then, snapping to his feet, Jim attempted to pin Clay, but when he left the ground, Clay's muscular legs clenched around him in a chop, catching Jim's collarbone. He hit the ground with the force of a fallen tree. His brutal strength pitted against Clay's agility would destroy them both if the fight continued much longer. Abruptly, he released his intent, ending the brawl.

Neither man won.

Exhausted, Jim lay in the sand, his thoughts spinning an encapsulated view of his life. He'd been knocked down and out more times than not, and with each bout, an equal playing field slipped farther and farther away, turning competitors into enemies who grew larger, more hateful, devious, and calculated as time went on…while Jim's passion slowly shifted into rage.

Why had the color of his skin never fazed Lou? The man reached through Jim's outer shell and touched his soul. Jim recalled him saying, "Those who have faced death often find their sense of values change." Is that what happened to Jim? Had his values changed when his dreams disintegrated into ash?

He knew that wasn't what Lou referred to, but Jim could pinpoint specific times in his life that gutted his resolve. Each one sparked a flame that burned hotter each day until the blaze of hatred burned in his belly...but he didn't want to live a life obsessed with rage.

He'd felt like an equal when he and Clay worked together to stay alive on the raft. What changed when they fell on dry land? Perhaps Clay's past altered his course, too. He shot a glance toward Clay who was still lying flat on his back and breathing hard. They accomplished so much...together.

Maybe the time had come to redirect his energy...to move forward in a different direction. He flashed on Martin Luther King, Jr. and the scope and breadth of one man's dream. Maybe God placed Jim here on this island to help him see a bigger vision...a dream that could change more than a single man...perhaps even a nation. He tensed his stomach, drawing forward into a sitting position, and a stab of pain shot through his core, acknowledging for days ahead he'd be sore and bruised from the fight.

Beaten and drained, Clay collapsed to the ground, gasping for breath. He laid motionless for several long minutes. When he finally staggered to his feet, he stumbled across the beach to the water's edge then dropped to his knees and splashed saltwater onto his face. The salt burned against his raw cuts.

A moment later, Jim stumbled toward the water then sat in the surf, allowing soft waves to wash over his wounds and rinse away the sweat. He shot a sideway glance toward Clay but said nothing.

Clay stood and shook his head then trudged toward the shack.

Body half leaning against a palm tree, Lou watched the brawl unfold, a stoic glare cast across his pale face and forefingers steepled, pressing against his lips. As Clay approached, he spoke, his words like a whisper on the wind. "What is so different between you and that young fella that you would beat him to prove you're…what? Superior?"

"Whoa, Lou. He jumped me first." Clay dropped to his knees and sat. "I simply returned the favor."

"And you did nothing to provoke him?"

Clay lowered his gaze and stared at the sand.

"I realize something in your past might have given you a skewed image of black folks. Sadly, that's more common than not. But for the life of me, I don't understand the inequality that taints our country. We fought a civil war to end that injustice. Black and white stood together when America fought two world wars. It's a crying shame we all can't treat each other as people… Americans…instead of dividing them into demoralizing groups." Shaking his head, Lou adjusted against the palm tree. "When I die—"

"No, Lou. I won't hear you talk about dying."

He frowned. "We all die, Clay. When our time comes. I'm at peace with how I've led my life. I

157

want more…but if my time is near, I have little to atone for." He lifted a hand and placed it on Clay's wrist. "Do you? If someone wrote about your life, are you proud of what they'd have to say?"

Lifting his gaze, Clay pinched his brows together. "I don't suppose anyone'd have much to write about."

"You have time, son, to make a difference." Lou squeezed Clay's wrist. "See people for who they are…their moral fabric…don't be blinded by superficial crap. We all bleed the same and we come together in greatness because of our commonalities…not our differences."

Again, Clay dropped his gaze to the white sand. He'd reacted to Jim's aggression, but his own actions only made the fight worse. Lou was right. Hostility fed rage and only served to divide them further. "His attitude grinds me like fingernails on a chalkboard. Sometimes I think he wants trouble."

"He's angry at the world…you heard his story…right? How would you feel?"

Clay nodded. He hadn't fooled Lou for a second. He went to bed because he realized where Jim's rage came from and had trouble looking through Jim's eyes. But the shack had thin walls. Lou knew Clay heard every word.

"Jim's a good man, Clay."

"I can't change the world."

"No, but you can make a difference, son. The Declaration of Independence promises equality to every American—" Lou tried to pull himself upward, but let out a tortured moan, closed his eyes and leaned his head against the tree trunk.

Clay popped up and snatched the morphine bottle lying next to Lou and gave him another tablet then adjusted Lou's position to ease the pain as best he could. Feeling Lou's pulse, Clay tensed his neck and shoulders.

Lou's skin was hot to the touch. His ashen face and pale lips were dry and sallow, and his eyes dimmed with a splash of red. He tried to hide the pain, but Clay knew his friend's condition was grave. Lou needed to drink some fresh water to combat dehydration and cool compresses to bring down the fever.

Clay lifted Lou's head and grabbed the canteen then dribbled a slow stream of water into his mouth.

Throughout the entire ordeal, Lou had complained very little. The morphine must have lessened his agony, but the man had guts of iron. There was so little Clay could do to help. Lou's injuries needed medical attention. Without a doctor, he wouldn't last much longer.

Opening his eyes a slit, he grabbed Clay's wrist. "Stop wasting your life crunching numbers. Change the world, Clay." His hand went limp.

Clay stared at Lou's chest slowly rise and fall. Thank God he was still breathing. Clay had to make contact with civilization to get help for Lou. Turning, he grabbed the radio and walked a few steps toward the water. He might have better luck away from the tree grove. But he wanted to stay close enough to keep an eye on his friend. Cranking the radio was one thing positive he could do…and helping Jim was another.

When Jim trudged toward him, Clay looked

up.

"How is Lou?"

"Not good."

Jim shook his head and plodded toward the oysters and mangos. He dug a pocketknife from the supplies then trudged several yards away before he knelt and began preparing breakfast.

Clay stood and strode toward him, rubbing his sore chin. "You have a damn hard punch."

"You have a hellava southpaw, yourself, Clayton...and your leg strength caught me off guard."

"It's Clay. No need for last names here. We're all friends, right? Do you think we could start over?" Lifting a hand, he offered it to Jim.

"For Lou's sake, I'll give it a whirl." Jim extended his hand, grasping Clay's with a strong grip and a firm shake.

Clay knelt beside Jim, and they prepared the food together. When they finished, they returned to the palm grove and served Lou some breakfast.

He fluttered his eyes and faintly shook his head.

Jim stared at him a long beat then knelt and picked out choice pieces of mango and oysters to tempt him.

Lou managed a bite, laboriously chewing and swallowing hard. But when Jim offered a second bite, he waved off the gesture, leaned over and retched. Energy obviously waning, he let his head drop and closed his eyes.

Jim fell back from his squat and began eating.

Sick at heart, Clay thanked Jim for helping prepare the food. As he ate, he watched his friend sleep. Though he'd known Lou only a few weeks, he felt as close to the man as he would a brother. The disaster bonded them…bonded all three of them…forever.

To escape his daunting thoughts, Clay stood. "You mind watching over Lou for a bit? I think I need a swim."

"Not at all…and thanks." He turned toward Lou.

Clay strolled along the beach, silently staring into the endless sea and the deep azure sky. The blazing sun burned his shoulders. Again, he slipped off his clothes then dove into the sparkling lagoon. The water swathed him with an odd, comforting cool warmth. After a lengthy swim along the coastline, he turned, face upward, and floated. Eyes closed, he allowed the waves to roll sensuously beneath him as they made their way to distant shores. The only sound was the muted song of seagulls gliding along the beach.

For what felt like an hour or so, he frolicked in the briny sea, occasionally diving below to explore shells and sea creatures scuttling across the ocean floor. Underwater, he felt as if he had escaped into another world. Myriad fish, none of which he could identify, swam in and out of the coral reef, creating a rainbow of color as they danced to their own silent tunes. Marine life here was so different from Savannah, yet both astonished and delighted him. Diving deeper, he explored crevices and valleys of the coral, careful to maintain a distance from whatever might lurk in the dark shadows below. Coming up for air, Clay saw the palm grove and shack in the distance. The escape relaxed him, but he wanted to check on Lou. He swam toward the shore.

Snatching his pants from the sandy beach, he yanked them on and winced...the pain was a clear reminder his fight with Jim would hurt for a while.

Chapter Twenty

Weeks had passed since Teri's accident, and still no word from Clay. Trembling at the thought of why, her stomach twisted. She wasn't sure what made her feel worse, being abandoned by her husband in her time of need or her injury. She thought about her last conversation with Rob.

"The magnitude of these assignments keeps the men quite busy. That paired with the remote location...I don't expect to hear from Clay any time soon."

Warm tears welled then spilled onto her bandages. "Did you send him a telegram about the accident?"

"I had planned to do just that, but you said you didn't want him to worry. "Rob took her hand in his. "You know he'd drop everything and come home if you needed him, but in doing so, he'd lose the clients."

"Yes. I remember. And I don't want him to

worry." The hollow feeling in her chest deepened, compounded by a sting of guilt prickling down her arms and legs.

Meg and Rob had helped her so much, handling everything she couldn't do lying in a hospital bed, household duties, bringing Teri whatever she needed from home, and taking care of the children. Having only recently moved to Houston, she would have been lost without them.

Rob was right, too. Clay would come home if he heard the news. This assignment involved important clients and would give his career a big boost. The last thing he needed was a sniveling wife who couldn't survive without him by her side.

When Teri's parents arrived from Atlanta, Meg said she and Rob had loved taking care of the kids so much they made a decision to have some of their own and would help Teri more if she needed them.

Teri's parents were thrilled to spend time with Emery and Jenny. But along in years, they brought Mattie, their live-in housekeeper, to care for the kids. Mattie had been with the family since Teri was a child and was an integral part of their household. Teri knew the children were in good hands. She smiled, recalling Mattie's promise to watch Emery and Jenny when Teri and Clay spent an anniversary weekend away.

"From the moment I laid eyes on yo' little babies, Miss Teri, I fell in love with them. I makes them behave, but I do for them whatever they needs, and spoils them something terrible."

The first time Teri's parents visited her at the hospital, her mother was so distressed over Teri's bandages, the doctor requested she stay away until Teri's condition improved. She stewed over the idea and fretted for a while but finally convinced herself she was needed at home to help Mattie with the children.

Teri's father, on the other hand, visited her every day. He had always been her rock, and this time was no different. He gave her hope, support, and soothed her frazzled nerves when she worried about Clay. Today, the doctor planned to take off her bandages, and Daddy promised he'd hold her hand during the entire process.

Apprehensive about seeing her wound for the first time, Teri grabbed the sheet and drew it to her neck. Her stomach tied into knots, but she didn't want her father to see the fear in her eyes. As soon as he stepped into the room, he chatted about this and that while they waited for the doctor, telling funny stories about Emery and Jenny, what they did in school, or when they took them to the park.

When she asked if she'd received any letters from Clay, her father shook his head and immediately changed the subject. She felt fortunate he still tried to protect her and didn't want her to dwell on something she couldn't change.

A sharp knock on the door sent a chill down her back. It was time to remove her bandages. Doctor Morgan and Nurse Stella walked into the room.

"Well, Mrs. Clayton. How are we today?" He snatched her chart from its hook and scanned the pages. "You look chipper this morning. Your father's company must be helping you heal. I bet you're ready to get these bandages off." He pulled a wheeled table to his side, placed some surgical tools on the surface then leaned over, clipped the gauze and began to unravel the dressing around her head.

Finally, she'd no longer look like the invisible man.

Again, he clipped the scissors and removed more gauze. When the dressing was almost off, he paused. "You do understand we expect to see some scarring. That means your body is healing. This kind of injury takes time. Don't be frightened when you see discoloration and swelling. When the tissue heals further, it will look much better. We'll consider if you need any additional surgery later. Okay?"

She glanced at her father then nodded.

Dr. Morgan peeled off the last piece of gauze.

Teri's gaze locked on her father. His reaction would tell her more than any mirror.

Squeezing her hand, he winced, then closed his eyes and turned away.

Teri's heart sank. She knew her face was repulsive. Thank God Clay was out of town.

Doctor Morgan cleaned the wound, closely examining the tissue then motioned to Stella.

Immediately, she snatched a hand mirror from the table and gave it to Teri.

Clenching her eyes tightly, Teri clutched the mirror to her chest. Then, drawing in a long breath, she gazed at her reflection and felt the blood drain from her face. She dropped her father's hand. A single tear rolled down her cheek, and the floodgate opened. Stomach retching, she let go of the mirror.

Stella caught the handle before the looking glass hit the floor. "Don't fret, Mrs. Clayton. You still need time to heal."

Teri scowled and jerked away then coiled into a fetal position and wrapped her arms around her knees. "No. That can't be me. How could you do this?" She moaned. "Go away. Everyone. Leave me alone." She yanked the sheet over her head as if hiding her face would make the scars disappear.

Doctor Morgan placed a hand on her shoulder.

Trembling, she jerked away. The sheet slid from her head and draped across her lap.

"We talked about this possibility, Mrs. Clayton. I've seen far worse scars heal quite well."

Her father sat on the side of her bed and drew her close. "Give yourself time, Teri. You have to have faith."

"The nurse will give you a sedative. Get some rest." Dr. Morgan rehung her chart on its hook.

Stella injected medication into her IV. "The scars will heal. Just give them a chance."

A sudden stream of warm honey rolled through Teri's arms and legs, soothing her nerves.

Her father eased her onto the pillow, still holding her hand. His eyes glistened as they too filled with tears.

Drowsy, Teri squeezed his hand. "Clay can't see me like this…please don't let him, Dad."

He released her grip then patted her arm. "You get some rest. I'll be back to check on you later." He stood and followed the doctor to the door and stopped him from leaving.

Teri closed her eyes, feigning sleep. But she

167

wasn't tired. She was heartsick.

Stella tucked a strand of Teri's hair behind her ear. "It'll be okay. You just rest now. Things will look better tomorrow." She turned and joined Dr. Morgan and Teri's father.

"It doesn't look too good now, but given time to heal, the wound won't be nearly that noticeable." The doctor reassured him.

"Shame about her face, such a pretty little thing," Stella said.

They strolled into the hallway and closed the door behind them.

Broken and alone, Teri cried herself to sleep.

Several days passed, and the swelling began to subside, but every time Teri dared to glance toward the wall mirror, she shuddered at her reflection. Now, staring at her image, she shook her head then lowered her gaze to the floor. Heartsick at the thought of her children seeing her…she imagined their reaction. Would she scare them? To her, she looked like a monster. She wondered if makeup would help hide the scarring enough for her to stand having anyone glance her way. The only person she would allow in the room aside from Dr. Morgan and Stella was her father.

When the doctor mentioned plastic surgery, Teri perked up. She would undergo anything if it might keep her from looking like this for the rest of her life. Hearing a knock, her gaze shot toward the door. She rushed across the room, slipped into bed, then she covered her face with the sheet. "Come in."

A candy striper open the door and stepped inside. Smiling, she held out a package.

Teri reached over the fabric and accepted the box. She immediately noticed Clay's handwriting. Since she knew Clay had no knowledge of her accident, she lifted her gaze. "Where did you get this?"

The nurse gave it to me. She said Mrs. Robinson dropped off the package and said she would stop by later this afternoon for a visit.

Teri sat straight, turning toward the window, so the girl couldn't see her face. With trembling fingers, she tugged the string until it gave way then unwrapped the package. Still shaking, she opened the little box and saw a pair of beautiful earrings nestled into the tissue. A shot of terror ripped through like waves of high-octane fuel. She snapped around then burst into a guttural laugh, tears trickling down her cheeks. She held them to her face. "See, don't I look beautiful?" She let out a vicious scream then flung them across the room.

Stunned, the candy striper backed away and ran into the hallway.

Teri stared at the earrings on the floor. Sunlight caught the blue stones, and they sparkled.

"He doesn't care enough to write...then this?" She sobbed and edged toward the window to retrieve the earrings. She grabbed them and held them next to the window then watched as a sunbeam danced through the facets and gleamed. "Oh Clay, come home. I need you." She lay back on the bed and cried, clutching the earrings against her chest.

Stella rushed inside and closed the door behind her then shuffled toward Teri and leaned against the bed.

Teri lifted her head.

The nurse's face softened, and she brushed the damp hair from Teri's flushed face. "Everything's going to be all right, honey." She put her arms around Teri and held her close.

Teri wept uncontrollably against her shoulder.

Stella patted her back. "You just go ahead, honey. Every woman has a time in her life when she just needs to cry."

Chapter Twenty-One

With no rescue or knowledge of the outside world, Jim and Clay cared for Lou, working together as the weeks droned on. Over time, they forged a deep and bonding friendship. They came to rely on each other, sharing duties, making sure the SOS was clearly visible at all times, cranking the radio, and tending to Lou with whatever was needed. But Jim's heart ached with each passing day. He knew the chances of Lou's survival dwindled with each passing hour.

This morning ebbed away slowly. Jim, in a sudden burst of energy, undertook the task of replacing the shack's thatch roof and thoroughly scrubbed the interior—as best he could with a makeshift palm leaf broom and saltwater. When he finished cleaning, he snatched the radio and carried it to the hard sand by the water's edge. Routinely, he and Clay took turns cranking a signal and praying someone would pick up the sound wave.

After turning the knob for what felt like at least

an hour, he stood and stared out to sea, hoping to spy some far-off vessel or aircraft making its way toward the island. He saw nothing but the endless sea vanishing into the distant horizon. Did the damn radio even work? His fingers grew stiffer and sorer with every day, and a new raw blister now stung the base of his forefinger. He dipped his hand into the waves, but the saltwater-burn only added to the pain. After flinging his hand back-and-forth several times, he peered at the open wound. He'd have to adjust his grip the next time he cranked the handle...but not today.

Jim grasped the radio and carried it toward the shack. "You can take a crack at it, Clay, but honestly, I don't think the damn thing works." He glanced at Lou sleeping on the tarp then blinked away. "You mind if I take a stroll down the beach?"

"Of course not, my friend." Clay smiled. "Go on. You worked your ass off this morning. You deserve some relaxation."

Jim shot him a nod, then strolled down to the water's edge and hiked toward the reef. Finding a familiar dune, he perched on the sandy mound and watched the breeze ripple across the quiet lagoon.

With a heavy heart, he thought about Lou and the many talks they'd had since the crash. Jim respected Lou and had forged a unique friendship with Clay. But what would happen when they returned to civilization? Tormented and bruised physically and mentally, Jim had done a lot of soul-searching over the last several weeks, trying to shed light on his rage and the endless battle he'd fought for most of his life. He lay back on the warm white sand and propped his head on his crossed arms. Staring into the azure sky, he pondered his life and imagined what wondrous things he might accomplish in the future once they were rescued.

The sun rose high in the sky and the beams warmed his face. At the same time, the cool waves lapped over his toes. A world of opposites existed everywhere around him, and he wondered how he might blend them together. Letting out a soft sigh, he stood, then plodded through the hot sand toward the shack.

When Lou awakened, Jim saw his eyes crinkle at the edges as he peered at both men sitting beside him on the tarp where he lay. He forced a weak smile that softened his pain-ravaged face.

When Jim offered him food, Lou shook his head. So, Jim pulled out his harmonica and played softly to comfort his friend until he drifted off.

Lou hated the fight between Jim and Clay, but after his initial reaction he said little more about it. Sometimes silence spoke volumes. He decided to leave the preaching to ministers. He simply asked Jim and Clay to take time and get to know each other. And they had.

Jim turned toward Clay, happy they'd made peace. Clay wasn't the superficial man Jim had initially pegged him to be. He was honest and had a good heart. The more Jim learned about Clay, the closer they became.

When the sun sank low in the west, it bathed the horizon in hues of gold and pink.

Lou moaned in his restless sleep and mumbled unintelligibly.

Clay bent over him then dropped to one knee and examined the deep purple bruises expanding around his chest and back.

Lungs barely inflating with each shallow breath, Lou's breathing labored.

Though Lou never complained, Jim saw the agony in his haggard face. When he checked Lou's pulse, the irregular beat worried him. With despair, Jim knew if help didn't come soon, Lou would die.

As if he heard Jim's thoughts, Clay frowned, his eyes mirroring the agony of Lou's suffering.

Watching the unspoken sadness between them, Jim's eyes pooled with unshed tears.

Clay blinked, holding his eyelids closed for a beat then raised his gaze to meet Jim's. For a long moment, their stare locked and something intangible connected between them without speaking.

As darkness crept in, Lou quieted, resting more peacefully.

Jim drifted into light sleep, keeping an eye and ear alert enough to help Lou should he need assistance.

For a while, the fire burned brightly against the jungle obscurity, but the flames slowly dimmed, leaving only glowing red embers and ash beneath the charred firewood. Within the forest, animals quieted their raucous calls, and the dense rainforest silenced except for an occasional rustling from the nocturnal creatures. The gentle surf lulled the island into sleep and waves rushed onto the lonely beach, stealing tiny treasures then swirling them into the deep blue sea.

Jim awakened the next morning early enough to fill several hollowed-out coconuts with fresh water from the falls. By the time he returned, Lou was waking up, so Jim knelt beside him and rinsed his face. When he finished, he sat on his calves and turned toward Clay.

Stretching, Clay yawned, then rolled to his side. "How is he this morning?"

"He's as hot as a pistol. Maybe a little delirious, too. I feel so helpless. This is the only way I know to bring down his fever, short of hauling him into the ocean."

"That's actually a good idea. His temperature has spiked off and on for the last few days. If he spikes again, let's carry him into the surf." Clay touched Lou's forehead then flattened his lips. "He's getting worse. Whether he has internal injuries or an infection, he needs a doctor."

Lou mumbled incoherently, lashing back and forth. His ashen face, haggard and sallow, sagged around the dark circles beneath vacant eyes, and his breathing was harsh and spasmodic.

"I'll get some more morphine." Finding the bottle, Clay popped open the lid then tilted it, letting the contents fall into his palm. "Only two tablets remain, Jim." Hesitating, he carefully returned one to the bottle then handed the pill to Jim.

After crushing the pill and taking care to avoid losing any of the precious powder, Jim opened

Lou's mouth and placed the particles on his tongue. Then he grabbed the canteen and, tilting Lou's head backward, he let a few drips trickle into his mouth to wash down the medicine.

Lou coughed and thrashed his torso from side to side. To keep him from hurting himself, Jim and Clay held Lou's shoulders firmly against the ground until the drug took effect. After a while, his rigid body relaxed and his breathing slowed to a more regular rhythm, but his pulse still beat far faster than normal. He opened his eyes briefly to see both men sitting beside him, one on each side. A soft smile curled the edges of his lips. Then he closed his eyes and dozed off.

Jim stood to fetch more wood for the signal fire then stepped into the shed and grabbed the radio. He set the device on the end of the tarp and turned the handle slightly. Hearing a clattering noise, he halted. "I still don't know whether this damn thing works or not after the storm. If it worked, I think someone would've found us by now. But we can't just sit here and watch Lou die. We have to do something."

Lou's head rested against Clay's shoulder, and his soft purr slightly wiggled his lips.

Jim shook his head. He didn't speak the words his thoughts envisioned, but he knew Clay had a similar image of his own.

Shifting his arm, Clay held Lou's head, then gently repositioned it. "Now that he's finally sleeping, I sure hope the rest numbs his pain."

Jim nodded then snatched the radio and paced several yards away to avoid disturbing Lou. He cranked the radio hard and gazed across the lagoon, desperate to take his mind off the inevitable demise of his friend.

The playful wind scudding across the water caught his attention in time to see two small sand-devils race toward each other, collide, then disappear into a sandstorm. For the first time, he took note of the beautiful splendor of this island paradise. Palm trees swaying reminded him of hula girls, and he cracked a soft smile at the thought.

Turning his view toward the jungle, he noticed brilliantly colored birds fluttering around the dark forest, chittering and squawking noisily as they awakened from the long, cool night. The taro plant with its dark green heart-shaped leaves wept silently, dripping dewy moisture onto the ground.

The sun overhead lost the crimson splendor of early morning and now beamed glittering gold rays against the azure sky. The shoal lay like a sapphire blanket over the coral reef and glistened as breakers tumbled across and exploded into a beaded spray— then disappeared into the sea. Banyan trees reminded him of long-limbed chorus girls caught in a ludicrous position by the snap of a camera lens. How did he not notice the magnificence of this hidden utopia?

Again, he gazed along the beach and saw fiddler crabs busily skittering along the water's edge, shadowing the outermost tip of each wave as they gathered their daily meals. Papaya blossoms mingled with the scent of various tropical flowers creating an exquisite aroma drifting through the air. An orchid trembled in the breeze, its petals opening

177

wide to embrace the sunshine. The beauty of nature he'd never noticed before amazed him. How long had Jim looked without seeing…heard without listening…lived without living?

Clay watched as Jim cranked the radio and gazed at the lagoon. He marveled at the man's resilience. Had his own skin been cast as dark, would Clay have held his course after being knocked down time and time again? What tainted the human soul to warrant such a class system, judging others by such insignificant standards like color? Born a white, Anglo-Saxon, Protestant shouldn't automatically mark a man as a golden child who could do no wrong, any more than a darker skin should brand a man inferior—or a scarlet letter cast a woman as an adulterer. In the scheme of things, Clay was simply lucky.

"Lucked out," a voice murmured in a husky whisper.

Stunned at the timely comment, Clay lowered his gaze to meet Lou's. "Did you—"

"Shh…I need to talk." He swallowed hard then licked his dry cracked lips. "This…is it for me…I've known…for a while…all torn up inside…" His voice faded.

"No, Lou. You have to hold on just a little longer."

His eyes lit up for a brief moment. "I can't complain…had a helluva life…while it lasted."

"Please, Lou. They're coming for us. You've

just got to have faith."

"I've made my peace...except...for one thing...need a favor."

"Anything you want, Lou."

His voice weakened, but his will wouldn't relent. "Tell...Ba...Bobbie I wanted...to keep our date...but I can't..."

Clay fought the tears filling his lids. "If the time comes, you know I will."

Lou fumbled with the ring on his finger until it slid off. He motioned for Clay to take it.

Clay opened his palm then stared at the simple gold design with a single ice blue diamond in the center. He could no longer hold back his tears. They streamed down his cheeks and fell onto the ring in his hand.

"Not what I planned...but tell her...the ring...to remember that one moment...for both of us." He closed Clay's fingers around the ring then lay back, drained by his effort.

When Clay opened his fingers, the sunlight caught the diamond in a blaze of blue and gold. He turned to see Jim standing close, tears trickling down his cheeks.

"He's not—"

"No. Thank God. He's just asleep. But his time is near." He switched his gaze to Lou.

"I pray someone picked up the sound waves and finds us before it's too late." He turned and paced toward the radio to continue his task.

Eyelids softly fluttering, Lou's head lay in Clay's lap.

Clay lifted him carefully and slid from

underneath then stood. Spying the canteen, he reached for a drink. The drone hum of mosquitoes buzzed close by and Clay spun to search for the swarm but saw nothing. The noise increased. Confused, he glanced skyward and saw a glimpse of silver in the clouds. "Oh, dear God." In a sudden burst of energy, he yelled out. "Jim, come here. Quickly."

The droning whir...it's a plane. Pointing madly toward the sky, he shouted out again. "Jim. Look."

Immediately, Jim dropped the radio crank and stood, his hand shielding the bright sunlight. Seeing the faint image, he waved his arms and jumped up and down to get the pilot's attention.

Dashing toward the beach where the SOS message beckoned skyward, Clay flapped his hands in the air and yelled at the top of his lungs. The big, dark blue twin engine had an American insignia on the side. Recognizing the aircraft as a Lockheed patrol jet, Clay watched the airplane swoop low in the sky then circle. When the pilot swung in low at the far end of the beach, a package tumbled from a small cargo sheet. The bundle plunged then thudded onto the sand. Again, the plane circled the island then shot away, returning in the direction from which it came.

Jim and Clay raced down the beach toward the package.

Clay grabbed a note taped onto the box and stuffed it into his pocket. After tugging the bundle to the clearing, he tore off the wrapping. Inside, he found several cans of soup, meat, coffee, medical supplies, blankets, cigarettes and matches. *Damn, someone actually found them.* They were finally going home.

Clay dug the note from his pocket. The pilot had scrawled a quick message to the stranded survivors:

Saw your SOS. Alerted Pago Pago. Seaplane capable of landing on the way.
Chin up!

Clay's gaze rose to meet Jim's. He snatched the package and darted toward Lou. Then, like kids opening Christmas presents, the two men yanked out blankets, cans, and metal utensils and placed them onto the tarp.

Jim shot a glance toward Lou. "They found us, Lou. We're finally going home."

"Just like I told you, buddy." Clay spread the cans next to Lou. "We have a feast here. What's your pleasure?"

Lou moaned softly.

Jim grabbed a pot, filled it with water, and set it on the fire for coffee. Opening a pack of cigarettes, he tapped one out, lit it, then offered the pack to Clay. The few cigarettes they saved were gone by their second day on the island, and Clay felt grateful to puff on a fresh one. He held it in the corner of his mouth, then grabbed the blankets and folded them into a bed for Lou. Placing them beside the injured man, he motioned to Jim.

They rolled Lou onto his side then slipped him into the makeshift bed. Lou moaned but didn't fully

181

awaken.

Jim ripped off the top of the coffee and poured a good portion into the boiling water. The aroma permeated the clearing.

As the magical scent finally invaded his senses, Lou mumbled.

Finding a cup, Clay poured the hot coffee, added a touch of cool water then raised Lou's head and held the mug to his lips.

He swallowed a few mouthfuls then stared at Clay. "Where's Ben?" He scowled. "And Bobbie On the plane…save her…please save her."

Again, Clay held the coffee to Lou, worried at his reaction.

After another few sips, he shouted, "Help…her." He coughed and sputtered. "Bobbie? Ben. Oh, God." The haze over his eyes cleared as the coffee warmed him. "Clay?"

"Everything will be okay, Lou. Help is on the way. You're going to make it, buddy. Just hold on a little longer. For Bobbie."

"So tired, Clay…too tired…no more time." He sighed softly and fell against Clay's shoulder, coffee dribbling from the side of his mouth.

Clay laid his head on the bed, then felt his pulse.

Lou's face muscles tensed briefly.

Laying his head on Lou's chest, he listened…but heard nothing.

Chapter Twenty-Two

T ears blurring his vision, Clay lifted the blanket over Lou's face.

Jim clasped a hand over his shoulder and squeezed, a veil of heartache distorting his features. He turned away and robotically poured a cup of coffee then offered the brew to Clay. They sat in silence for several long moments. Grieving over their loss, they consoled each other, recalling their most memorable conversations, and how much they'd learned from Lou. Together, they vowed to take Lou's spirit and wisdom with them to fight for the soul of America.

In the distance, the soft whine of an airplane whirred louder and louder as the rescue craft approached.

Clay stood. "We'd best gather together our possessions. The seaplane will land soon."

Rising, Jim scanned the camp area and shook his head. "There's nothing to gather—except Lou." He ambled into the shack and gazed around then turned toward Clay. "Perhaps we should pack the gear and tuck it into a corner of the shed—in case another castaway takes refuge on this island." His gaze lowered to the still body of his friend hidden beneath the blanket. "We might have saved Lou…if we had those supplies. I'd like to believe we could save someone else one day by leaving emergency provisions behind."

Heartbroken, Clay nodded then dropped to his knees. Gathering together an armful of supplies, he carried them into the tiny hut. Touched to the core by Jim's response and suggestion, Clay wondered how he ever thought less of the man. The color of his skin was no more important than the color of his hair or eyes. Again, he questioned what devil lurked in the heart of men spewing judgment on others for nothing more than the tint of their skin?

America was forged from collective wisdom and a mighty premise—his thoughts flashed on the Declaration of Independence he'd memorized as a child. At the time, the words meant little more than a mundane homework assignment, but now he pondered the meaning.

We hold these truths to be self-evident, that all men are created equal, that they are endowed by their Creator with certain unalienable Rights, that among these are Life, Liberty and the Pursuit of Happiness.

America broke free from the British, declaring their freedom. They fought to abolish slavery and to expand that freedom to every American. A chill shot down his back like a bolt of lightning…what if Clay survived the crash for that purpose…to somehow remind this country their forefathers fought and died to secure those unalienable rights for our posterity?

A plane sputtered as it swooped overhead, and Clay turned toward the clamor, shielding his eyes from the bright sunlight. He watched the Amphibian aircraft settle onto the lagoon then taxi toward the beach.

Jim dragged the last of the supplies into the shack then stood next to Clay.

"We'll be home before you know it." Clay shifted his gaze toward Jim. "I learned a lot on this island from both you and Lou. I'm sorry for how I treated you."

Jim shrugged. "I gave you little reason to change your mind." He held out a hand. "I hope we remain friends when we return to our lives."

Clay clutched Jim's wrist and held it tightly until Jim responded by wrapping his hand around Clay's. After a firm shake, Clay pulled him into a hug. "Lou would be happy we're friends, as am I. We finally learned what he tried to teach us."

"Hey fellas, you two need a ride stateside?"

Clay turned to see two men trudging toward them through the sand, carrying a stretcher.

The pilot, wearing an aviation cap, a khaki shirt, and trousers, offered a handshake. "You two survivors from the jetliner crash several weeks back?"

"Yes, sir." Clay smiled. "And as many times as I've longed for an island paradise, I'm anxious to get home."

The second man stepped forward. "Looks like you two men are the sole survivors of that flight."

185

Dressed in navy blue, he wore a stethoscope around his neck. "The pilot said he saw a third man when he passed over earlier who appeared injured." He scanned the palm grove. "I guess he was mistaken."

Jim sighed. "Sadly, our friend couldn't wait. He passed shortly after the plane dropped supplies." He tossed a glance to Clay. "But we'd be beholden if you'd bring him along. Lou was a good man and a better friend."

"And we promised we'd take him home." Clay motioned toward Lou's body and took the lead "He's precious cargo, fellas. The only thing of value we'll be taking with us."

They rolled Lou onto the stretcher, then lifted.

Jim stepped next to Lou, standing erect as if at attention. He silently clasped a hand over the side of the stretcher.

Clay immediately followed suit, grabbing the opposite edge. "Lou was a man among men and deserves the best care possible."

Together, they all carried the stretcher to the aircraft like pallbearers then stepped aboard and lay him gently against the bulkhead.

A few minutes later, the plane taxied over the clear water before turning into the wind. Shoving the throttles forward, the pilot picked up speed. Waves beat a rapid tattoo against the hull until the aircraft lurched, taking them airborne.

Heading into the sun, the pilot made a wide sweeping turn to the south, then headed toward Pago Pago…and home. In silence, Clay reflected upon his time on the island and how both men came to be so important in his life. Hours passed, and the sky darkened. Stars twinkled on a velvet black backdrop as the plane soared onward.

When they reached their destination, multi-colored lights winked on and off along the runway below. An ambulance met the plane as they landed. Clay and Jim were rushed inside and chauffeured toward the American Samoan hospital. The siren shrieked until they pulled in front of the entrance. Clay and Jim were wheel-chaired into examination rooms where bustling nurses took charge, jabbing and poking as they checked vitals, weight, and examined every inch of their bodies.

Once Clay was released, he found Jim and, after several phone calls, they'd made arrangements to send Lou home.

"I guess this is it." Clay extended his hand toward Jim and gave him a strong shake. "I feel as if I'm saying goodbye to my brother. Please, don't be a stranger, Jim." He dug into his pocket and drew out a folded piece of paper. "This is my address and phone number. If you ever need anything...even if you just need to talk, please call me."

Jim accepted the note. "I will." He paused a beat. "You and Lou changed my life. I'll miss you, brother. Thanks."

"For what?" He pinched his brows together. "I gave you nothing but grief."

"Perhaps. But I dished out as much as I took. Lou broke through my anger...and you showed me it's possible to change. The rage I held did nothing but feed a fire already blazing. Hate breeds hate. Rage breeds rage. It's time cooler heads prevailed."

Clay lowered his gaze to the floor. "I'm afraid

187

our country needs more than cool heads." He raised his gaze to meet Jim's. "I'm just not sure what one man can do."

"Ah." Jim chuckled. "My daddy used to say, 'if I was king, the world would be different.' Since neither of us will likely be king, I reckon we take change one man at a time. Take care, my friend."

Clay patted Jim on the back. "You, too. Until we meet again."

They turned and went their separate ways.

To his surprise, Eastern Airlines paid the tab for whatever Clay needed: food, lodging, taxi service, and air flight to go home. Exhausted, he still managed to eat a thick steak, medium-rare with English peas and a baked potato with sour cream and butter. After dinner, he checked into a hotel to get a good night's rest.

Finally, he was in a quiet and private place where he could sit and call Teri. She must have been frantic at the news of the crash. By now, she likely thought he had died along with everyone else. According to the Amphibian pilot, the rescue team gave up the search weeks earlier, presuming the entire crew and passengers aboard the flight had perished. Clay needed to break the news gently to his wife.

He propped a pillow under his head and laid on the bed...what a wonderful piece of furniture. He took a moment to relish the feeling before raising the phone receiver and dialing his number. The phone rang and rang, but no one answered.

He checked the clock and determined the time in Houston then placed a person-to-person call to Rob at the office. Again, the line rang and rang with no answer. He transferred the call to the Robinson home, but like his two previous attempts, there was no response.

Chapter Twenty-Three

S eated at his highly polished mahogany desk, the Texas Senator pensively pulled at his upper lip. In front of him lay a copy of the afternoon paper, carefully folded with a picture at the top. In the background, a phone rang incessantly but, so deep in thought, he scarcely noticed the chime.

The phone halted for a long moment of silence then rang again. This time, the sound penetrated his thoughts. Lifting the receiver, he leaned back in his chair. "Emery Clayton."

Jenny's voice twittered on the other end of the line.

Clay listened for a moment, smiled, then acquiesced. "Anything for my beautiful daughter. Just sign my name on the tab."

He returned the phone to its cradle then shifted his gaze to the paper and studied the picture.

Jim had aged, but so had Clay over the last ten years. He glanced at the wall mirror and noticed

191

how his dark hair mingled with silver streaks, especially around his face, and the late afternoon sun beaming through the window highlighted the silvery strands. His face gave the impression of a man in his prime, but he could swear his eyes carried a burden with the knowledge of centuries.

Again, he glanced at the newspaper photo of his old friend, and memories swirled from the dusty corners of his mind. After their rescue, he and Jim returned to the States, and lost touch, but Clay never forgot the few weeks that changed his life forever. He gave Jim his address and phone number, hoping they would remain close. Filled with delusions of grandeur, Clay wanted to change the world. He would never be king, but he could run for office and little by little, he would teach others what he learned.

As a Congressman, he introduced bills stressing equality. As Governor, he opened doors of hope and blocked prejudice and hatred. Now, a Senator, his dreams materialized with political influence.

He thought about Jim often and wondered what became of his brother's dreams. When they parted, Jim disappeared into the crowd, strengthened with renewed resolve—and today's paper validated his thriving mission.

Apparently, Jim worked his way through a passivist organization run by Martin Luther King, Jr. A lot of white folks respected the organization. Clay felt sure Jim had much to do with the group's progress.

He laid the paper on his desk then gazed at his watch. Close to five-thirty...time to head home. He slid some papers into his desk and turned the lock. Standing, he folded the newspaper once more and tucked it into his briefcase before strolling out of his office.

His secretary, just finishing her day's work, glanced up and smiled as he walked past her desk.

"Goodnight, Miss Adams."

"Goodnight, Senator. Have a nice evening."

Snatching his Stetson from the stand, he strode out the door and closed it behind him. The moment he stepped outside, the oppressive heat slapped him, and he jerked at his tie to loosen the knot around his neck.

Slipping behind the wheel of his black Chrysler, he started the engine. The air-conditioner hummed, blowing in his face as he pulled out of the parking lot and onto the street. The drive home spun his thoughts to an all but forgotten time. Passing his old office reminded him of the bridge game Teri and Meg set up for the evening. Luckily, he moved in and out of traffic with ease and would be home with plenty of time to spare.

Pulling into the driveway, he stared at his house, a large red brick home set well off the road. A long velvet lawn stretched across the front with deep green grass, reflecting the care his gardener lavished upon the grounds. The hedges, kept well-manicured, were freshly clipped, and the flower display exploded with color.

Every time he drove into the driveway, Clay relished the reality that he actually owned this elegant home. The house fit their social status, which was the only thing that kept Teri happy these days—a sad truth he wished he could change.

He parked then opened the door, stepped into the heat, and stretched.

A small boy ran from the front porch to greet him.

Opening his arms to his son, he twirled the child several times before lowering him to the ground. Forgetting his cares for the moment, Clay laughed, dropped his briefcase and hat and hugged his boy. Then, catching the child around the waist, he swung the boy down through his legs and over his head then around again until they both fell onto the grass dizzy and laughing.

A Yorkshire terrier shot from the front porch. Clay stood, arms open, as the dog hopped into his embrace. Moochie twisted, wiggled, barked, and jumped, happily joining in the fun. Then he reared up on his tiny legs and pawed at Clay for more attention. Kneeling, Clay nuzzled the terrier's ear.

The boy gazed at his father. "You mustn't pet Moochie, Daddy. He's been bad today. Mother says he can't come into the house anymore."

Clay chuckled. "Tell me, Lou, what terrible thing has Moochie done? No, let me guess. He ate all of the cake Mattie made for our dessert. No? He forgot and left the water running? Did it flood the house and carry everything away?"

Lou let out a little giggle. "No, Daddy, you know…what he always does."

Clay gazed at the small dog and sternly wagged a finger.

"Moochie, you didn't leave a present on the floor again, did you?"

The dog shrunk to the ground and put his paws over his eyes.

Clay laughed then tousled Lou's blonde hair. Angling his head, he saw a tear escape and roll down his son's cheek. "Come on now, it can't be that bad. I'll talk to Mommy and see if we can't get Moochie a reprieve. But if I get him in mommy's good graces, he'll have to promise to behave."

Lou's face broke into a smile. "Oh, he will Daddy, I promise."

Clay bent down to grab his Stetson, and Lou jumped onto his back and threw his arms around his father's neck. Holding his legs, Clay bumped him along as he galloped to the door. His son laughed with pleasure and implored Clay to trot around the yard.

After doing his bidding, Clay lowered Lou onto the porch and handed his hat to Mattie.

Lou ran toward the car and quickly returned, tugging his father's briefcase, his face red with exertion.

Mattie watched them with an affectionate smile. She placed his Stetson on the rack and went about her chores.

Just as the door closed, Moochie sneaked through the entrance.

Mattie glanced over her shoulder and glared at the pup, raising a brow.

Clay put a finger to his lips. "Shhh."

Snickering, she rolled her eyes and shook her head.

As if knowing he wasn't in Teri's good graces, the pup shot up the stairs and out of sight.

"Miss Teri is in the library," Mattie said.

"Thank you." Clay sniffed at the aroma arising from the kitchen. "Umm. Something sure smells good. I can't wait until dinner." He turned and strolled into the library.

Sitting at the desk writing something, Teri lowered her pen and raised her head.

Clay strode across the room, bent over, and attempted to kiss her.

She turned her face, so the kiss landed on her cheek. "Really, Emery, your distasteful exhibition in the front yard was frightful. A man in your position can't afford that kind of display." She shook her head. "Besides, you spoil that boy to death."

Clay dug his fingers into the back of the chair then turned and peered out the window. "Lou tells me Moochie is in the doghouse again."

"That animal stained our new ivory rug. I've told Lou time and time again, if he must keep the dog in the house, he must be responsible and take the animal outside to do his business."

Clay paced toward the liquor cabinet. Thankfully, Mattie had fresh ice waiting and ready. What did he ever do without old Mattie?

Taking two glasses from the shelf, he mixed some cocktails. "I'll talk to Lou, dear, and see what I can do to help him understand." He paused and shook the martinis. "He's so young, Teri. Sometimes he just forgets."

"Then he is too young to have the animal." She shot a harsh glare toward Clay.

His stomach tightened. "Please, let's not go into this now. I'll teach him a sense of responsibility."

Again, Clay shook the drinks then poured the martinis into the glasses. After sipping one to avoid spilling the contents, he placed the other cocktail in front of his wife and softly kissed the top of her head.

Gaze shifting to Clay, Teri picked up the glass and took a sip, her sour expression twisting her features with a chord of discontent. "You'd best change for dinner." The faint scar on her cheek barely showed beneath the fall of her hair. "Don't forget we play bridge with Rob and Meg tonight."

Clay nodded. He ached inside. Teri rarely smiled these days...not like the girl he married so many years ago. He downed his drink as he left the room and walked toward the stairs.

Sitting on the third step of the stairway, Lou watched him leave the library—a room Lou wasn't allowed to enter.

Clay strode toward him. Smiling, he quietly motioned for his son to follow him upstairs.

Lockstep with his father, Lou marched after Clay into his bedroom and plopped onto the counterpane.

Removing his suit coat, Clay hooked the garment on the back of the door. Running a hand over his chin, he groaned at the prospect of another shave. He ambled into the bathroom and Lou shadowed him.

At the buzz of the shaver, Lou imitated Clay, pretending to shave his face.

Clay chuckled. Just watching Lou put him in better spirits. After he finished his shave, he strolled into the bedroom, unbuttoning his shirt. As he changed clothes, he chatted with Lou. He hadn't the heart to scold the boy. But he impressed upon him the necessity of watching the puppy and making sure Moochie went outside from time to time. Lifting the boy from the bed, he lightly patted the seat of his pants and sent him down to Mattie, reminding him once more to keep Moochie out of trouble and, for the time being, out of sight.

Lou smiled then skipped down the stairway.

Clay listened to his son's receding footsteps as he knotted his tie. From his closet, he drew out a sports jacket, flipped off the light, and returned to the library.

Teri had already left the room.

Clay wandered to the liquor cabinet, mixed himself another martini then sat in the chair his wife vacated. The silent room, now darkening with the setting sun, relaxed his angst. Sipping his drink, he paused and swirled the liquid, his thoughts on Teri.

She had a hard time adjusting to the scar on her cheek and isolated herself from everyone except Clay, Jenny, and Emery. At first, she clung to Clay. But after Lou was born, she began to socialize and made friends with a lady's group. Relieved she was finally getting out and making friends, Clay encouraged her involvement. But over time, she hardened, and her bias deepened. She never forgave the black boy. When he threw a can at the window, he shattered more than glass. Teri's self-confidence splintered as well, and the socialites she befriended fortified the prejudice.

Clay gave her all the support he could muster and constantly told her how beautiful she was. But she recoiled and turned away. What did he do wrong? As time passed, she showed little interest in him and no patience with their children. She barely interacted with the family, leaving child rearing to Mattie and Clay.

Jenny, now a young lady of sixteen, with light brown, curly hair that framed her pixie face, appeared content, but Clay knew she needed her mother's attention.

Emery, on the other hand, was a serious teen, who preferred a book over sports and rarely played ball. His dark eyes and tanned face were so like Teri's.

His two older children got along okay, but Lou relied more on Mattie than his own mother. Named after Lou Rosson, Lewis Emery Clayton was a big name for such a small boy. Clay smiled at the thought of his youngest son.

Teri's distance gnawed at Clay. Dear Lord, how long could his marriage go on this way? He'd survived a plane crash and being stranded on a deserted island for weeks on end, and he came through the ordeal a stronger, more passionate man. Why did Teri's accident have an opposite effect?

Swirling the contents in his glass, he thought how very much he loved his wife. The darkness surrounding him kept his thoughts churning. He heard Emery come home, but the library door remained closed. Not until Mattie called from the dining room, announcing dinner, did Clay respond. He chuckled. No matter how many times Teri threatened her, Mattie still called out to announce the meals. He stood and placed his empty glass on the desk then strolled into the dining room.

The moss-green drapes hung full-length to the floor, and the walls were painted candlelight ivory with a brown and green leaf pattern scattered throughout. Mattie truly went all out tonight. The table was pristine, with an ivory lace cloth and candles flickering from silver candlesticks.

Jenny and Teri were seated and waiting when Clay entered the room. He pulled out his chair to join them.

Emery strode in, head down, buried in a book.

When Clay cleared his throat, his eldest boy immediately closed the hardback and slid into his chair.

Clay gazed at Teri. She looked as young as the day he married her, and the candlelight hid the discontent that usually tensed her lips.

Teri shot a glance at Lou's empty seat and raise an eyebrow.

A heartbeat later, Lou scooted into the room and took his place at the table.

Clay lowered his head. *"Bless us oh Lord, and the food we are about to receive. Thank you for these and all our many other blessings. In Christ's name, we pray. Amen."*

An echo of Amen followed the prayer. Clay placed his napkin across his lap then reached for Lou's and tied it around his son's neck, bib-fashion.

Mattie strode into the room with a tossed salad in hand and served everyone an appropriate portion.

Lou grimaced, but bent over his plate and took a bite.

Jenny burst into conversation. Between forkfuls of food, she told her mother about the wonderful dress her father gave her permission to buy earlier that afternoon.

When Mattie served the main course, Clay gave her a grin and a wink of thanks for preparing his favorites. She beamed.

Later, Mattie served the dessert, placing a huge piece of cake in front of Lou smothered with icing.

Teri barely spoke during dinner, but didn't miss the opportunity to scold Mattie for spoiling Lou. Then she turned to Clay. "Please show respect for Rob tonight. You never know when you'll need a favor from a friend."

Clay stabbed at his cake. "Meg and Rob are good friends, Teri. I wouldn't want them any other way." Gazing down, he saw the tablecloth flutter then Moochie's nose, but it promptly disappeared under the table.

Teri followed his line of vision and gazed down, but apparently saw nothing.

As soon as they finished their dessert, the children excused themselves.

Clay stood, and hearing Mattie mumbling to herself, he wandered into the kitchen.

"Best meal you've ever made, Mattie."

"I declare, I just don't understand that woman. Can't she see that she cuts you to pieces when she acts like that? Makes a body wonder…." Her tirade was interrupted by the front doorbell. She put down the dish towel, but Jenny's voice floated from the hall.

"I'll get it, Mattie, I'm right here."

201

"Bless her sweet little soul. All three of them are such good children. I just can't understand their mother."

"It's fine, Mattie. She's had a lot to deal with. She just needs time."

Shaking her old gray head vigorously, she took out the anger on her dish towel, swiping it dangerously across the dishes.

Moochie scrunched farther into his bed. The house was not yet safe for a small puppy to frolic freely.

Chapter Twenty-Four

J enny opened the door to greet Meg and Rob.

"Jen, you look more beautiful every time I see you. How's my girl getting along, honey?"

She smiled. "You're just a sweet talker, Uncle Rob." She called out to her parents. "Daddy, Mother, Uncle Rob and Aunt Meg are here."

When Clay and Teri came to the door, Jenny leapt upstairs.

Clay waved a hand toward the den, where they sat and talked for a while before dealing the cards. They had just started the second hand when Mattie waltzed in with Lou in tow, scrubbed and ready for bed.

Making the rounds, he kissed everyone goodnight, then gave his father a big hug before padding back to Mattie. He slid his little hand into Mattie's old dark one. "Will you tell me a story, Mattie?"

"Oh, child, you know I will." She laughed and

led him up the stairs. "What story do you want to hear tonight?"

After several hands of Bridge, Teri rang for Mattie to bring refreshments. She returned with freshly brewed coffee, still steaming, and four slices of chocolate cake.

Rob leaned back in his chair. "I saw the newspaper today and saw a fella by the name of James Rucker. Isn't he the black man who survived the same Eastern Airlines crash as you?"

Clay raised his gaze to meet Rob's, surprised he remembered Jim's name after all these years.

"Yes. Jim was stranded on the island with me and Lou for weeks."

Meg turned to Clay. "He has some really sound ideas, don't you think?"

Clay shot a glance toward Teri, his response directed more to her than Meg. "Yes, he has some wonderful ideas, Meg, and I'd like to help his group as much as possible. A lot of southerners talk about integration, but most don't lift a finger to help. Jim's organization brings social awareness to the foreground and helps social acceptance more than all the other organizations combined."

"When he speaks Monday," Meg said. "I hope he gets a great response to his innovative ideas. The education programs he wishes to introduce will help our city tremendously, don't you think?"

Teri broke in heatedly."I have no reason to champion the efforts of a colored man."

Meg and Rob silenced.

Shortly after Teri's comment, Meg said they needed to get home early.

Rob shook his head and groaned. "Meg pie, somehow I have a feeling you opened Pandora's box."

When they left, Teri turned on Clay. "I don't care what you think of Rucker. He's black. I hope you have enough gumption to not talk that way in public. There are names for white people who love the coloreds and once you get labeled, our whole family will be outcasts."

Clay turned to see Mattie standing at the door. She slumped and walked toward them, gathered dirty dishes then trudged into the kitchen. When the door swung shut behind her, he frowned. "Teri, you've said enough. Don't bring up this subject again."

"I've said enough?" She glared. "I haven't even begun. What did the blacks ever do for you? Don't you care what that black man did to me?" She yanked her hair from her face to show her scars.

"That was an accident, Teri. And he wasn't a man. He was a sixteen-year-old kid. That's Jenny's age."

"He learned how to act from his people."

"Perhaps. But if his people made enough money to live on, he wouldn't have stolen a can of beans."

She stomped her foot. "He could have killed me. As it is, I'm disfigured for the rest of my life."

"He didn't mean to hurt you, Teri. He didn't even mean to break the glass. He just threw the can to escape the authorities. Yes, he acted impulsively. But most kids act impetuously."

"You still have no idea what I went through."

"Okay, let's look what the blacks did for us, if Jim hadn't helped me after the plane went down, I wouldn't be alive, here with you and the kids. I would never have made it to the island or survived alone."

He held her shoulders squarely in front of him. "Teri, think about everything Mattie has done for this family."

"She's done what she has been paid to do."

He stared her straight in the eyes, "For God's sake, Teri, Mattie helped raise you…she loves you like a daughter, and she gives our children the love and attention you couldn't give them."

Her eyes blazed with anger. "Love?" She almost screamed. "What do you know about love? You're always so calm, so right, so…oh, I don't know. You aren't the man I married. I've been living with a stranger for the last ten years." She wrenched away, flew up the stairs and slammed the bedroom door.

Clay's hands dropped to his side. He stood in silence, staring at the stairs for several long moments. Turning, he opened the front door and stepped outside then closed it quietly behind him.

The air had cooled slightly, and a soft breeze played in the trees overhead. Remembering the pup, he opened the door a crack and gave a little whistle. A moment later, Moochie was in his arms, his tail wagging and playfully licking his cheek.

Clay closed the door and scratched the pup's ears, finally understanding what led to the emptiness in his marriage.

Chapter Twenty-Five

T he next morning, Clay awakened early and went for a walk, making sure to let Moochie tag along. Now, he sat in the library, reading his mail. He could hear Mattie, busily working in the kitchen and the noises upstairs told him the children were awake, but Teri complained of a headache and chose to stay in bed.

Sifting through several bills and personal letters, he came across a small package wrapped in brown paper. A hotel box number in the left-hand corner took the place of a return address, and a stamp announced the parcel was insured. Wondering who on earth might have sent the item, he ripped the paper, then opened the box.

Pulling aside the tissue, he looked inside to see a small brown doll with long black hair. He immediately recognized the souvenir. Someone had worked long hours to smooth the snarls from the doll's hair and wash the soil from the flowered muumuu. Clay's hand trembled as he lifted then carefully examined her. For the second time within twenty-four hours, old memories flooded his mind. Seeing a note tucked inside the box, he opened and read the missive.

Dear Clay,

I am sorry I failed to write to you the past ten years. I guess I needed time to sift through all the hatred that burned in my gut. The last three years, so much has happened. If only all men could face death like us and come to terms with themselves as we did.

Sometimes it seems too great a job to accomplish my dreams. But God works in mysterious ways and usually where there is the greatest need. Surely, others will carry on if I should fail. I'm embarrassed to say I kept this doll. It was rightfully yours. At that time, I needed something more tangible than a memory. I'm sure you understand and hope you forgive me.

I have a request I'd like you to consider from an old friend. If you have the time, I'd appreciate an appointment so I could talk with you about an urgent matter. If not, please meet me for lunch while I'm here as I would like to shake the hand of my very dear friend.

Sincerely,
Jim Rucker

Clay laid the letter on his desk, last night's argument still ringing in his ears. He spoke his true feelings about helping the blacks, but what could he do? His wife burned with anger and was vehemently against everything he now believed. Her conjecture regarding their friends was probably true. He would be labeled and so would his family. How would helping Jim affect his marriage? In his position, a senator needed to remain diplomatic.

Again, he picked up the little doll and stared at the gift that was meant for his six-year-old daughter. Memories of the time he'd spent on the island swirled through his thoughts.

A tap drew his attention. He opened the door to see Mattie.

"Mista Clay, breakfast is ready."

He stood and silently followed her into the kitchen. The passion he'd felt on the island burned again in his belly.

Mattie straightened the curtains in the library then wandered to the desk. Laying aside the mail and a gift box holding a small doll, she dusted the surface. Curiosity getting the best of her, she picked up the toy and mused over where the doll came from. Returning the gift to the box, she saw a note on the floor. Wondering if the paper was meant for the trash or had mistakenly fallen, she leaned over and picked up the note and set it on the desk. Her gaze froze on the signature, Jim Rucker.

Seeing no one in sight, Mattie did something she never did before. The fight between Mista Clay and Miss Teri still fresh in her mind, she read the letter from start to finish then whispered, "That man caused enough trouble in this family just by the mention of his name."

She finished the cleaning as quickly as she could. Having promised Lou she'd take him to the park that afternoon, she still had lunch to fix. But she decided a phone call was more important. She'd take care of that matter first.

At three o'clock, Mattie was finally ready to go. She perched her little black hat securely onto her gray-haired head and stuck in a hat pin to hold it in place. She fetched her mending bag and tucked her purse deep inside where it would be safe.

"Come on, child. It's time to go." Taking Lou's hand, she marched them off the porch and walked three blocks to the park.

Lou skipped all the way, tugging her arm to hurry her along. When they got to the playground, Mattie sat on a bench and watched Lou wait his turn for the swings. She grabbed her bag and rummaged through the clutter for her sewing. For an hour, she sat busily, while Lou played on the equipment with his friends. Occasionally, she glanced at the path until a well-dressed man approached her. He stopped at the bench. "Madam, are you Mattie Birch?"

She nodded. "I is."

"I'm Jim Rucker. I believe we have an

appointment."

"Yes, Mista Rucker. Please, sit." She patted the bench beside her then cinched her face. "I needs to tell you 'bout Mista Clay and Miss Teri. She be his wife…and when you and Mista Clay be lost on dat island, Miss Teri, she be hurt bad."

Jim frowned. "I'm aware of Clay's wife and family…and I'm sorry his wife was hurt…but what does that have to do with me?"

"Miss Teri, she be at the market when a black boy stoles some food. When da manager caught up to dat boy, he flung a can right through a windah next to Miss Teri. He didn't mean her no harm. He just be hungry. But dat glass cut Miss Teri's face somthin' awful…the scars still be on dat sweet girl's face…but they be on her inside, too."

Jim shook his head. "I didn't know that, Mattie. And I'm sorry, but why are you telling me about this story? I can't change history."

"You seems like a good man, Mista Rucker. And I knows you and Mista Clay be friends. Mista Clay say he learnt a lot on dat island 'bout black folks…and he wants to hep you make this country better…but Miss Teri be so sad and hurt…she blames black folks for everything now. That family is so tore up… if Mista Clay get involved—"

"I understand. You think if Clay helps me, his marriage will suffer."

She lowered her head. "Yes." Lifting her gaze, she stared directly into his eyes. "So, you see, Mista Rucker? Mr. Clay, he loves his wife…and he has a fierce passion to hep black folks. He's a good man, and I hates to see him all tore up."

He placed a hand on her shoulder. "Don't you worry, Mattie. I'd never hurt Clay. I won't involve him in anything that would jeopardize his marriage."

Lou ran to the bench, breathless from playing tag, and stared, first at Mattie then at the man she sat next to. Holding out his hand, he spoke in a very adult voice. "I am Lewis Clayton—but my daddy calls me Lou. I'm pleased to meet you."

Jim stared at the small boy. "Your name is Lou?"

"Yes, sir, what's your name?"

Jim reached out his big brown hand and shook the hand the child offered. "I'm Jim Rucker, Lou. I knew your father many years ago. You look a lot like him."

Lou's face beamed at the mention of his father. Lifting the child to the bench, Jim set him on his knee. "Lou is a great name. Do you know who your daddy named you for?"

The boy grinned. "I'm named after my uncle." He lowered his chin and gazed at the ground. "He was killed in an airplane crash, so I never got to meet him, but Daddy said he was the bravest man he ever knew."

A wide grin splashed over Jim's face. "Well, as it happens, I knew your daddy's friend, Lou. He was my friend, too. And your daddy was right. Lou Rosson was the bravest man I've ever known...but did you know your daddy was very brave too?"

Lou's eyes widened. "Really?"

"Why, sure he was, and the best friend a fella could have. You're a very lucky boy to have a daddy like yours."

An ear-to-ear smile swept over Lou's face.

"Your father is a fine man. If you work real hard, maybe you will grow up to be just like him." Jim stood and tipped his hat. "A pleasure to meet both of you. I'll be seeing you." He turned and strolled down the pathway.

"I'll be seeing you," Lou called after him.

Mattie rose and gathered her things then held Lou close, hoping she did the right thing by talking to Jim Rucker.

"Who was that man, Mattie?"

"A friend of your father's, honey. When you get a little older, maybe your daddy will tell you all about him. We best be goin' home. It's time to start dinner."

Lou nodded, but was quiet on the way home. When they got to the house, he squeezed her hand and whispered, "I don't think Mommy would like Daddy's friend. But if Daddy likes him, so do I."

Mattie smiled. "You are such a smart boy, Lou. I think you're right. Maybe we should keep Mista Jim our secret for the time being." She tussled his hair and took him inside.

Casi McLean

Chapter Twenty-Six

A large stone church, set well back onto the lot, spread over a vast area of the block. Shaded from the hot afternoon sun, the chapel stood under an old magnolia tree. Inside, a young woman waited, making last-minute adjustments to her long white bridal veil and train. Dressed in an ivory wedding gown, she stood with bridesmaids gathered around her, busily smoothing her dress and tucking wisps of curls around the pearled halo that caught her train.

The lovely bride waited patiently. No one noticed the slight tremble of her hands holding the bouquet. When the wedding march began, a sharp knock rapped on the door and she stepped forward. A man escorted her down the hall.

Mis-stepping, she quickly matched her timing to that of the escort by her side. He held her arm tightly for a moment then led her down the aisle of the chapel.

Sprays of flowers adorned the front of the

215

church with one yellow rose set into the greenery. Behind the altar was a stained-glass window depicting scenes of the life of Christ. The sun shone through into a blazon of brilliant colors.

The bride carried a small white Bible adorned by a single orchid. Guests oohed and ahhed as she passed by on her way to the altar. A flurry of whispers broke as she took her place beside the man waiting. From all indications, she was calm and serene. Such a lovely bride.

The minister raised his voice and started the traditional ceremony, "Dearly beloved, we are gathered here to join this couple in holy matrimony."

Again, the bride trembled and gazed at the man beside her, a handsome man with strong features and gentle eyes.

The bride knew she loved him, but her decision about the marriage took a long time. A ray of sunlight caught the ring on her right hand, a man's gold ring with a brilliant blue diamond set in the middle. Her eyelashes flickered as she gazed at the treasured ring. She would never forget what the ring meant. A moment in time she shared with a man who held her heart. He meant so much and always would, but it was time to let go.

Ten years had passed before she found someone else with whom she wanted to share her life. She turned her head slightly and peered at the ring he now held in his hand. They exchanged vows, and the minister pronounced them man and wife. He lifted her veil and kissed her lips ever so softly. Tears of happiness welled until they spilled onto her cheeks. The organ rang out with the wedding march, and the happy couple swept down the aisle in a flood of excitement and good wishes.

The guests filed out of the chapel and lined the walkway, waiting for the newlyweds to leave for their honeymoon. The bride and groom stepped out of the church and paused. He turned to face her.

"Are you ready, Bobbie?" He held out a hand.

She smiled and nodded then squeezed his arm. "I can't wait to start our life together. Let's go."

They ran through the crowd of spectators in a shower of rice and waved to their families and friends, then hopped into the car and drove away, a trail of shoes and empty cans clattering behind the car and a big sign on the trunk that read: Just Married!

Casi McLean

Chapter Twenty-Seven

Clay tried to reach Jim all afternoon. By four o'clock, he considered driving to Jim's hotel, but he attempted one more call. He listened as the switchboard operator rang Jim's room and heard the phone buzz in the background. This time, he would give his friend plenty of time to answer. After at least twenty rings, Jim finally picked up the line. "James Rucker."

"Jim? This is Emery Clayton. I received your package. Thanks for returning Jenny's doll. The souvenir brought back a lot of memories. I'm delighted to hear from you after all these years and would love to catch up."

"Absolutely, Clay...hey, about my note—"

"I'd love to help you, Jim. I'm not sure what you need, but I'm certainly open to suggestions. Can you stop by my office? Your hotel is actually quite close by."

"I'm free anytime you can squeeze me into your schedule."

Clay glanced at the clock on the wall. "How about right now?"

"Are you sure? I don't want to impose."

"Good friends are never an imposition, Jim. My address is 801 Yale Street. Just tell my secretary who you are, and she'll bring you right in. I'm looking forward to seeing you."

"See you shortly, then."

He hung up the receiver and sat back in his chair. Business papers in disarray, he rifled through them then straightened them into a stack. Clay still was undecided on what he could do to help his old friend without exploding his marriage, but he'd find a way once he heard what Jim had in mind.

Ten minutes later, Miss Adams buzzed his intercom announcing Jim's arrival and showed him into Clay's office.

Clay stood, scooted around his desk, and held out a hand. "Jim, so nice to see you." He gripped Jim's hand and gave it a firm shake. "I see time has been kind to you. You don't look a day older than the last time I saw you."

"I'm not sure I believe that bunk, but thank you for the compliment."

"Please, sit." Clay motioned toward a leather wingback chair then slid into the matching adjacent seat.

"A lot of water has rushed under the bridge since we last parted. You've made quite a name for yourself, Senator."

Clay smiled. "You've done all right for

yourself, too, Jim."

After exchanging a few pleasantries, a long moment of silence ensued.

Jim shifted positions and crossed a leg over his knee. "I know this might come as a surprise considering my—shall we say—vehemence regarding the subject, but I've learned insisting on equality might not be the right battle to fight." He paused a moment then continued. "Thanks to Dr. King and a few others, a lot has changed in ten years. Where we have achieved equality, many blacks don't know how to move forward. I believe the future of our race—of our country—depends entirely upon education."

"I completely agree." Clay leaned forward and rested his forearms on his knees. "Assuming a man's talent is the best qualified for a particular job, hiring or promoting an employee should be given on merit, nothing more and nothing less."

Jim nodded. "But prejudice still rests in the souls of many. Hate will still drive decisions and hypocrites will follow the status quo only to the extent necessary to avoid criticism. Prejudice takes time to evaporate." Jim tapped his fingers on the side table. "We need to produce an equal playing field with our counterparts, so employers see us as people...as excellent candidates for a job...instead of classifying us first as Negroes. That is our race's real goal."

Clay readjusted his position. "For my money, the employer's only interest should be his profits and his stockholders." He rubbed his thumb and forefinger on his chin. "I think you've hit on something big, Jim. You want to be judged as individuals within the population. Focusing on the need to be equal, you'll always stand divided...always be working to attain equality." Clay stood and paced by the window. "Something Lou said to me on the island struck me like a bolt of lightening...and it has stayed with me all these years...to be truly equal, society needs to see everyone as a part of one population...no tags or categories. Only by taking away the divisive categorization will you ever accomplish real equality."

"Exactly. Lou taught me those words of wisdom, too, and after years of fighting for equality, they finally made sense."

"He was an amazing man."

"That he was, my friend." He paused and drew in a long breath. "That's why education is so crucial. I recognize raising the standard of education for blacks is paramount. But we can't stop there." Jim stood, placed a hand on the back of his chair, and shot a gaze out the window. "The country must see our entire population as Americans instead of splitting individuals into divisive categories. Regardless of why one group of people might be set apart from others—whether the conflict-ridden feature is skin color, hair color, religion, gender, education, or any other reason— the separation sets up a potential for conflict, which can be used to divide our nation as surely as slavery did. I believe by seeing everyone as American, each individual will be characterized by merit and achievement...and we erase America's caste system discrimination."

Clay leaned against the front of his desk and crossed one foot over the other. "Brilliant...and I agree blacks need to be educated to compete on a level field...but...you're missing half of the equation."

Jim raised his brows and approached Clay. "How so?"

Snapping his fingers, he locked a stare with Jim. "The whole country needs education, Jim. They need to learn—just like you and I learned on the island—united together we make the country stronger."

Jim nodded. "It is only when men rise above accepting the status quo that they can conceive of the concepts of morality, honesty, patriotism...and liberty and justice for all Americans." He smiled and clasped a hand over Clay's shoulder. "But understand, I have no intent to level an accusing finger. I only want to provide quality of education to every American for future generations."

"Of course." Clay rubbed the stubbles on his chin. "In actuality, the Constitution guarantees our society will always have millionaires and paupers, under the premise that success and failure falls where it will—but once all individuals receive equal opportunity to drink from the same learning well, the division in the country should dissolve. So, you aren't requesting anything that isn't already promised in our Constitution. People somehow forgot what we stand for...we just need to remind them."

Jim nodded then gazed at his watch. "I'm sure

I've talked way too much. I don't mean to push my passion on you. I live and breathe this agenda...but I don't have a family, Clay...this dream is my child."

"Well, from what I've read recently, you are doing a remarkable job." Clay paused to study Jim's demeanor—and the man he had become. "You know, Jim...because of Lou...and you...the meek accountant you met ten years ago became a politician. I decided I needed a voice to shout to the world my grand discovery. Now, as you might suspect, I have connections from the Chamber of Commerce all the way to the President of the United States, and I will speak to whomever I can to get your idea heard."

Jim stood. "I'd never ask you to do anything you feel uncomfortable doing...or involve you in anything that would jeopardize you—personally or professionally. You understand that, right?" He held out a hand.

Clay reciprocated and grinned. "Yes. I know you're a good man, Jim. And thank you."

Jim's gaze caught a glance of the pictures Clay had on his desk. "This must be your family."

"It is...I think Jenny is a bit too old for dolls now, but she'll love the sentiment of the little muumuu figurine."

Jim smiled. "The two boys look a lot like you." He hesitated then spoke, "Clay, I have already discussed this with some of the members of the Board of Directors. From their comments, my vision promises to get rather ticklish. You don't have to get involved."

"Nonsense, Jim, I want to help, and you inspire me to be a part of this." As he said those words, his thoughts spun to Teri. She would not be happy with his decision. But Jim lit a spark within Clay that had hidden beneath burnt embers and ash for far too long. If he'd never met Jim, he would have never become a senator.

Somewhere on that south sea island, between Jim and Lou, Clay found inside the man he wanted to be. He worked hard the last ten years to achieve a voice that could be heard throughout the country. A voice that would calm a burning society and heal a broken nation. If he didn't help Jim…his life and everything he believed he stood for would be a lie.

Chapter Twenty-Eight

C lay glanced at his watch as he pulled into his driveway. Almost seven p.m. He parked and stepped out of the car onto his plush green lawn.

Mattie greeted him at the door with a fresh glass of tea, a mint leaf floating atop the ice.

"Has the rest of the family eaten dinner?" He handed her his hat and suit coat then took several swigs from the glass.

After setting his Stetson on the rack, she draped the jacket over her arm. "I took care of the children, Mr. Clay, but Miss Teri, she say she want to wait til you come home to eat. Your dinners are warm in the oven. Should I fetch them for you and Miss Teri now?"

"No, Mattie, wait until Teri comes downstairs. I don't know what she has planned."

She nodded and strolled into the kitchen.

Clay emptied his glass and followed her. Flipping around a ladder-back chair, he straddled

227

the seat and leaned his arms on the back. "I'm sorry you heard our little tiff last night, Mattie. Teri has held that anguish inside since her accident, and her torment finally erupted. She didn't mean what she said."

Mattie picked up a towel and dried the children's dishes, answering Clay without making eye contact. "Now, don't you worry 'bout that, Mr. Clay. Miss Teri been suffering somethin' awful since her accident. Her words didn't bother me at all. I know who she be inside."

"Having built up so much rage over the years, she doesn't see how much that anger has changed her. But her anguish shouldn't be directed toward you or any other person, black or white." He rolled up the cuffs of his shirt to the middle of his forearms. "I'm sure you heard me mention Jim Rucker last night. He's in town for a few days. What do you think about his plans to build a new school in this area?"

Her back facing Clay, she dried her hands then placed the dishtowel on the counter. "I think we needs something like that, Mr. Clay. I sure do. I can't say most white folks will think kindly of the notion, though. Feelings run pretty deep here. It sure would take some fancy talkin' to convince the white folks."

"Did you know Jim asked me to help with the project?"

Mattie frowned. "Guess I did hear something to that effect, Mr. Clay. You ain't gonna do it though, are you?"

"At my request, Mr. Rucker came to my office

late this afternoon. I told him I would do whatever I could to help."

She frowned. "He had no right to ask you for help, Mr. Clay. You can't get yourself involved." Mattie raised her gaze. "You needs to think about the family…how helpin' that man would affect Miss Teri. And Miss Jenny be seein' such a nice boy…what would his folks think?"

Surprised by her vehemence, Clay squeezed his brows together. " Jim wants to get rid of social stigma…so blacks, whites, and all colors in between are viewed as people? And I agree. Division, regardless of whether the divide is race, religion, creed, or gender can only hurt our country. You know that, right, Mattie?"

"I ain't had it so bad, Mr. Clay. We needs to accept the way life is. Youngins' comin' up don't want to work for anything. They want everything be gived to them for nothin'. They don't know a body just keeps workin' and tryin'."

"You're right, Mattie. That's why we need to bring up our children respecting everyone…not separating everyone according to the color of their hair, their height… or their skin. When I look at you, I see a good, hard-working woman. I'd rather have you as my friend than a lot of white people I know. You're part of our family."

"And I loves you all just like you was my very own. Please don't do nothing to hurt this family, Mr. Clay. That Rucker fella shouldn't of wrote a note like that."

Clay stood and pushed away the chair. "How did you—"

Lou burst into the kitchen. In his small cupped hands, he held a grey-tailed cardinal a bit too tightly. Feathers ruffled, the bird lay quiet and still. "He's hurt, Mattie. Can you make him feel better?"

She took the small bird, holding it gently in her chubby black hands, and examined it. "This baby have a strong heartbeat, honey child. He be flyin' again soon."

Lou ran from the kitchen then returned a few moments later, a shoebox clutched in his grimy little hands.

Mattie grabbed several sheets of paper towels from the roll by the sink and crafted a small nest. Then, she gently placed the frightened bird into the box and carried it outside.

Clay stood at the back door and watched her teach his son.

"Where should we put it?" Mattie scanned the backyard.

"Will he be all right, Mattie. Will he live?" Lou's voice quivered.

"Honey, s'pose you tell Mattie what happened to the little bird. He be pert near scared to death. Did a cat get him? Poor little thing."

"Nobody hurt the bird, Mattie, he got hurt all by himself. He flew smack into the sliding glass doors and fell to the ground. I thought he was dead. Will he be all right?"

Mattie put the box on the table at the edge of the pool, near the hedges. "Silly little thing, fightin' shadows, he was."

"How do you fight shadows, Mattie?" Lou wrinkled his nose. "Have you ever fought shadows?"

"Child, I reckon everybody fights shadows at one time or another. That little bird has a nest somewhere close by. He picked our very own yard for his home and was taken care of his babies, just like yo momma and yo daddy take care of you. He be a good ol' daddy bird, out getting dinner to bring home. He just saw himself in the windah and thinks it be a big bird tryin' to get to his family."

Lou let out a chuckle. "But, he didn't really see a bird. He saw himself, Mattie."

"That be true, but he don't know about that, honey. He looks at that windah and he sees somebody trying to cause trouble."

Mattie raised her head and saw Clay still standing in the doorway. She turned toward Lou. "You think that little ol' bird silly, fightin' himself like that, honey?"

Lou nodded.

"There aint' nothing God ever done better than to have daddies take care of their youngins'." She raised an eyebrow and gave a quick gaze toward Clay.

"But there wasn't another bird for him to fight, Mattie."

"They coulda been honey. They coulda been."

Clay turned and stepped into the kitchen then glanced over his shoulder.

Mattie patted Lou on the head then followed Clay inside. "Mr. Clay, I do somethin' I want you to know 'bout."

He faced her, pressing his brows toward his hairline.

"I...I read the letter that Rucker fella wrote...then I call him. I know I shouldna do that, but I did. He say it didn't matter if you help or not. He say he just push until he get that school built. Mr. Clay, he said he wouldn't ask you to help if it hurt Miss Teri."

"She'll be fine, Mattie. I promise."

Teri called from upstairs. "Clay, is that you?"

He stepped into the foyer and gazed up the stairs. Seeing her door ajar, he knew she'd been listening to his conversation with Mattie. "Yes. I'm home. Mattie says you waited to have your dinner. Shall I tell her you'll be downstairs shortly?"

"Yes. She can put dinner on the table. I'll be there in a few minutes."

The doorbell rang behind him. Clay spun then peered out the glass sidelight to see Jenny's date. He opened the door. "Come in, Woodrow. I'm sure Jenny is expecting you. She'll be ready in a few minutes. Let's have a seat in the library." Clay led the way then turned to the liquor cabinet, chatting with the young man while he mixed drinks for himself and Teri. "How are you and your father and mother, Woodrow?"

"Just fine, sir."

"I haven't seen them lately."

"Dad's been real busy this last week."

Clay chuckled. "Playing golf?"

Woodrow smiled. "He plays a good bit of golf, but that isn't what's kept him busy lately."

"Oh?" Clay turned to face the young man.

"Dad's upset over some school the blacks want to build. He and a group of other men want to fight the project. You know Dad."

Clay paused a moment. "Yes, I'd forgotten how deeply he feels about black people."

Woodrow nodded and chuckled. "I'm afraid this time he's out for blood."

Jenny walked into the room.

She looked lovely in her new dress. "Where are you two going this evening?"

"Diane's mother is hosting a party at the country club, Daddy. It sounds simply divine. They hired a band and everything."

"That sounds like fun." He paused. "Woodrow, my daughter's curfew is 11:00 p.m. You will have her home on time, right?"

"Oh, Daddy." Jenny rolled her eyes.

"Jenny, nothing good ever happens after eleven at night."

The teenagers looked at each other.

"The party ends at midnight, sir."

Clay spoke seriously, "Then you'll have no traffic leaving the event. Eleven sharp."

After kissing her father, Jenny called upstairs to Teri. "We're leaving for the party now, Mother."

"Have fun, dear," Teri replied. When the front door closed, she appeared at the top of the steps dressed in a clinging, white-silk lounging gown and silver shoes.

Clay had never seen her look more beautiful.

"Mattie...hold off on that dinner for a while."

"Yes, sir, Mista Clay."

He took the stairs two at a time and followed her into her adjoining bedroom.

Teri sat in the front of her mirror and began

brushing her hair.

He edged closer and put a hand over hers then took the brush and pulled it through her long dark hair, watching her face in the mirror. "You look like you did when I met you with your hair down like that, Teri. I like it. Why don't you wear it like this more often?"

Teri lifted her gaze to meet his through the mirror. Ignoring his question, she looked deep into his eyes. "I'm so sorry for last night, Clay. I shouldn't have said all those ugly remarks I don't know what gets into me sometimes. I feel so much anger inside I want to strike out and hurt whoever is close. I think all that rage exploded last night."

"Do you really feel I'm as awful as you said?"

"You haven't done anything wrong, Clay. You're always so calm, so right, so perfect... Oh, I don't know. Everything I do is wrong. I'm mixed up inside. If you would just once show you need me..."

"Need you? Oh God, Teri, I love you and need you more than you could ever know." Reaching down, he tangled his hand in her hair. Gently tugging her head back, he slid a hand onto her cheek and kissed her hard with the hunger of ten long years.

Disengaging herself after a moment, Teri picked up the brush and, again, ran it through her hair. Smiling, she murmured low, "Later, darling. Why don't you mix us some martinis?" Drawing her hair together, she gathered the strands and tied them with a white ribbon.

Clay hesitated for a moment and started to speak, but instead, he turned and went downstairs to fix the drinks. It had been so long…and he wanted her more than she knew, but not this way. They'd slept in separate rooms since shortly after Lou was born. At first, because after twelve hours of hard labor, the doctors had to cut Lou from her belly. She needed to heal. But over time, the distance between them grew. Both Clay and Teri changed from their traumas, and he had no idea how to mend the rip in their marriage.

Holding two drinks in his hand, he paused…then set the glasses on the table and walked toward the kitchen. Poking his head inside, he saw Mattie. "We'll be downstairs in a few minutes. Can you please bring our plates into the dining room?"

She turned toward him. "I'll set the table right now."

"Thank you."

When he returned, Teri was sitting on the loveseat. The lamp behind her made a halo over her hair.

"It's late, Teri. I hope you don't mind, I asked Mattie to serve dinner." He offered her a crooked elbow, and they strolled downstairs and into the dining room. He pulled out her chair then helped her push closer to the table. He barely had time to seat himself before Mattie served their dinner. Clay ate like a horse, and he was pleased Teri acted strangely content, more like herself than she'd been in years. After dinner, they wandered into the library.

"How about making us a couple of stingers?" Teri gazed at him through her lashes.

He couldn't help but wonder why her attitude suddenly shifted...and they rarely drank alcohol after dinner. Not wanting to make waves, he mixed the drinks.

She stood then waltzed across the room and changed the records to some old favorites. After turning the lights low, she sat on the couch.

When Clay heard "Stardust" fill the room, he knew Teri meant to seduce him. It was their song. Why else would she play that particular tune...and set the ambiance to such a seductive mood? He had longed for a chance to get closer for years. Could he jeopardize that now? He held out a hand. "Will you dance with me?"

She nodded and smiled.

They danced closely in the dimly lit room. Holding her tightly, Clay drew in the scent of her delicate fragrance. He paused and kissed her then guided her onto the couch.

She laid her head against his shoulder and drew her feet close. The silken material clung to her body, showing the outline of her sensual figure.

Clay leaned close and planted a kiss on her forehead. "Teri, you are as beautiful as the day I married you."

Her body tensed. She pulled away then stood and stepped toward the window.

"What's wrong, darling? Did I say or do something to upset you?"

She turned to face him, tears streaming onto her cheeks. "I'm not beautiful, Clay. I'm horrible."

"I don't even notice the scars, honey. They mean nothing to me. I see you as my beautiful wife."

She stared, frozen and rigid for a long moment, then placed a hand on his cheek. "You really mean that, don't you?" She spun then stepped toward the window and stared outside. "I'm the horrible one between us...did you know I intended to use everything within my power to seduce you tonight? I wanted to force you to give up on the idea of helping that man...your friend, James Rucker. But I can't seduce or manipulate you. Not now." She turned to face him. "I'd forgotten how much I truly love you."

Clay chuckled and rolled his eyes. "Inconsistency, thy name is woman." He stepped closer. "I knew what you had in mind, Teri, and I prayed you wouldn't go through with your seduction."

She frowned. "You didn't act like you knew. You were so sweet and—"

Clay pressed a finger onto her lips then replaced it with a kiss.

"Until tonight, I didn't understand why you'd choose to help a black man...especially after what happened to me." She ran a hand through his hair. "You changed after the crash, Clay. You never fussed over my injury or shared my anger at the boy...or the race. And I resented blacks even more for that. I'm still uncomfortable with your involvement...but I want to change, Clay."

He drew in a deep breath and whooshed it out, thankful she finally was willing to see things through his eyes. He wrapped his arms around her waist and held her close.

237

She drew back and gazed into his eyes. "You don't understand, Clay. I hated the world...but you didn't...all your hatred sank into the ocean with that airplane. The trauma...and the time you spent on that island...your attitude was so foreign. At least I thought it was...until tonight. When you told me how I look made no difference...I realized the depth of your change. Your eyes are open to see people beyond their physical appearance, be it scars..." She peered upward into Clay's eyes through her lashes. "...or the color of their skin."

Clay had never thought of his transformation that way, but Teri was right. He no longer saw people on the surface. Instead, he saw them for who they were inside.

Taking Teri's hand, Clay led her upstairs. Holding her close, he whispered tender words softly in her ear. She blushed like a bride and followed him—this time into *his* bedroom. Clay closed the door behind them.

Chapter Twenty-Nine

After finally making progress with Teri, Clay expected he'd sleep like a baby. Instead, he tossed from one position then turned to another. Only after hours of pondering how he could help Jim and keep Teri happy at the same time did he drift into a restless slumber. His eyelids twitched and his muscles jumped as he lived a nightmare...a dream where he was President of the United States. He stepped into an elevator, but the shaft had no floor. He plunged downward at a nauseating speed into an ominous darkness. He heard people screaming all around—people only Clay could save. They grabbed at him as he plummeted down the hollow shaft.

In a deafening crash, his flight thrust into an ocean of briny water. Gurgling as air bubbles surrounded him, he gasped for breath, struggling to free himself from the suffocating stench of jet fuel and death. Now, a seatbelt restrained him, held him captive in a watery grave.

Fingers cold and trembling, he felt for the catch

then tugged and heaved until he yanked open the latch. A whoosh propelled him upward until he burst through the surface.

The salty taste of blood surpassed that of the saltwater. Head aching, he reached for his forehead. The warm, thick substance trickled from the gash into his eyes and blurred his vision. He wiped a sleeve across his hairline to absorb the stream, and he winced in pain as the rough material scraped across his wound. Panic-stricken, he spun, gazing in every direction.

Again, he heard the screech of terrified screams…the pain and terror lurking in the darkness surrounding him. His hands flew to his ears to shield them from the voices.

"My death is near," Lou called from behind.

Clay swirled around but saw only darkness. "Lou, where are you?" he shouted, but no noise fell from his lips.

In the distance, he saw an island. Where was Lou? Clay stretched his hands forward but grasped only air as he once again slipped into the sea.

Jim grabbed Clay's wrist and yanked him from the ocean's grip.

For a moment, Jim's face twisted into a grotesque image…his arm ever slipping from Clay's grasp. Jim strained to reach out, but he couldn't catch hold of Clay. Screaming, as if in agony, Jim begged Clay to take action before the tide stole him too far to rescue.

Clay's head slipped underwater. The sound of his own voice gurgled as the nightmare forged a deathly grip. "No," he shrieked then lunged forward with everything he had. He grabbed Jim's hand, and together they pulled until Clay could feel the sand beneath his feet. Drawing his head upward, he saw Lou leaning against the shack.

"Your time has come," Lou called out.

Clay trudged toward him. "Hang on, Lou. I'm coming...I'll save you."

"You'll save them all," Lou replied. "It's your destiny."

Lou's image faded into a light blue mist.

Clay turned toward Jim just in time to see a hazy blue cloud whirl around his friend.

Feet sinking into the sand, Clay relented to the fog. In a violent swirl, he was lifted into the clouds. His limbs numbed. His neck ached...then silence consumed him.

Feeling drugged and weak, Clay forced his eyes open a slit then lifted his head and gazed around the dusty attic. Rubbing his neck, he twisted and stretched to dissipate the tension still gripping his body.

He gazed at a tiny window above then stood and peered outside. Dawn had broken and the first rays of light now filtered through the cobwebs stretched across the window. Gazing downward, he saw a flurry of activity. He glanced at his watch—five-thirty a.m.—he wiped the sleep from his eyes then cracked open the tiny window.

"POTUS is missing? How long?"

"I don't know, sir. We're looking everywhere.

He's not answering the redline, and no one has seen him since he retired last night."

"That's preposterous. We have far too much security in place for POTUS to go missing."

"Yes, sir. I know, sir. But Mrs. Clayton called. She said his bed was untouched—which happens from time to time when he has a lot on his mind— but she checked his office then called his private line. She says he's nowhere to be found."

"He's here, somewhere. Perhaps he doesn't want to be found. Stay calm...and check the tunnels."

The president...is missing? He scratched his head. Again, he gazed around the attic. A sudden surge of anxiety flushed through his body like ice in his veins. His hands flew to his cheeks...he ran his fingers over his face and hair then peered at his clothes. A distant memory flashed of an old looking-glass propped against a few boxes near the attic door. He scuttled through the loose boards at the back of the storage closet then dodged boxes and antiques until he stood in front of the mirror. After brushing off years of dust, he stared at the reflection. Emery Clayton—the third—returned his stare. Had he merely fallen asleep? If so, how could the reverie feel so real? His thoughts shifted back and forth from past to present. But nothing solidified...he ran a hand through his thick brown hair, and a chill prickled his arms. He had no idea how he was retrieved from the past...or why...but one thing he knew for sure—Emery Clayton, III, President of the United States, was finally home.

Chapter Thirty

Frozen in place, Emery inspected his reflection. From all indications, he simply awakened from an extravagant dream. In a whirl of nausea, forgotten memories flooded his thoughts. He stared at Emery Clayton, III—President of the United States. Stunned at his mirror image, he realized he hadn't aged a bit...he marveled that the life of Emery Clayton Senior still lived within his mind.

Frantic voices from the White House lawn grew louder. Emery crept toward a window and peered at the frenetic activity. How much time had passed in the present since his shift into the past? A day...a week...a month? Perhaps he returned to the present in an instantaneous loop... to the exact moment he left. After accepting his journey through time was real, anything was possible. The process might have drained his energy enough to initiate sleep as a means of recovery. Regardless of how or why the switch in time occurred, he—the President—had to reappear—and quickly.

Thoughts spinning to make sense of the incredible incident, he tiptoed to the Resolute Desk. The last thing he remembered before he slipped into the past was reading aloud the inscription carved into the wooden drawer and the bluish mist that swirled around the room. He ran a palm over the smooth surface until a finger touched the etched surface. Instinctively, he patted his jacket pocket for his glasses then perched them on the end of his nose and read the inscription—this time mindful not to speak the words aloud—

"God grant me wisdom to light the way and the strength of our forefathers to save the day."

Somehow, those words transferred his mind or soul into the body of his grandfather. A shiver swirled down his spine, and he trembled. The event made no sense. If someone told him about the miraculous time shift, he'd never believe it possible——and yet, he knew the transfer occurred. As President, Emery thought it prudent, at least for now, to keep his magnificent experience to himself.

From what he gathered watching the frenzied activity on the lawn, the Secret Service and staff appeared panicked, but his whereabouts must have only recently been in question. All things considered, he decided to slip quietly back to his quarters. He slipped from his refuge then crept down the back stairs and stole through the residence, carefully peering through each room and hallway before he entered.

No one expected him to be in the attic, as everyone appeared to be searching downstairs. Without being seen, he slipped into his private bathroom, locked the door, then he turned on the shower. After stripping off his clothes, he slid under the warm cascade and relished the sixteen-inch rain showerhead he'd totally forgotten about. He looked forward to having twenty-first century technology again, and he prayed he'd recall how to use it.

Running a soapy netball over his skin, he thought about Teri and the children—until a wave of vertigo slid a vision of Kathleen into the foreground with Madison and Savannah standing beside her. A wave of guilt pierced his heart. God, how he missed them. He ached to see his family after all the years he'd spent away. Memories streaming now, he envisioned the night he sneaked away to his attic haven and vanished into the blue haze.

After days of pleading, Kathleen finally acquiesced and took Savvy to Madison's graduation—without Emery. Another swell of remorse twisted his stomach. *Oh, God. His daughter's graduation. How could he brush aside such a milestone in Madison's life?* The night he plunged into the past, his marriage was in turmoil and skating on thin ice.

Social media had lured his girls into danger. They needed their father. Consumed with juggling his family and the demands of the presidency, he thought he'd explode if he couldn't find some peace and quiet to come up with answers?

Ever since the election, Emery's focus held steadfast on helping his country recover from the massive division strangling the nation. The temporary position gave him four years—at most eight—to reverse the devastation. He entered politics with the purest intentions to help the country he loved. But Emery never realized the depth of deceit or the unfathomable amount of money that drove the discord.

Lies, suspicion, and fearmongering inserted through social media, ripped at the fabric of the nation—all in the name of power and greed. Only hours ago, intelligence confirmed Emery's suspicions with solid proof, identifying the foreign nationals who initiated the power grab. But what cut Emery to the core was the secret list they exposed—a list of Congressional and Senatorial elected officials who sold their souls to the enemy. Bought and paid for, they furthered the division, spewing hatred and malice to the unsuspecting populous.

Again, Emery's thoughts shifted to Kathleen and the girls. They knew going in the sacrifices they'd face would challenge the family's resolve—and they charmed the nation with their elegance and posture. But, behind the pomp and circumstance, lending Emery to the country proved harder than they ever imagined. With the nation divided and a world in chaos, the lion's share of the weight fell into Emery's lap, and he found no time to consider anything else.

When he escaped to the attic, the pressure of the threatening war had hit a pinnacle. A massive blow was about to explode on the nation, and he had twenty-four hours to make a decision of monumental proportions—the impact of which would change the course of history.

Turning off the shower spray, he reached for a towel and wrapped it around his waist then padded into his bedroom. Choosing a dark blue suit, a crisp white shirt, and a red tie from the closet, he dressed, then gazed into the mirror, trimmed his beard and combed his hair. His reflection seemed so surreal. Could he jump back into his presidency as if nothing had happened after living his grandfather's life for the past ten years? He prayed no one would notice a difference in his behavior.

Clasping his hands together, he squeezed them tightly and drew in a long breath, then released it and strolled toward the window. The pristine White House lawn almost sparkled in the sunlight, reminding him of a distant memory. Gazing across the rich green grass, he considered what he'd learned during his time slip.

The fated plane crash that took so many lives and left three very different men stranded on an uncivilized island changed Jim and Emery's lives forever. He'd never forget what Jim once said: *If only all men could face death like us and come to terms with themselves as we did.* Facing death—and a little nudge from Lou—awakened Emery and Jim to what's really important in life.

History wrote of the nineteen sixties as a tumultuous period. Black pitted against white, the United States entered the Vietnam War, the Soviet Union's missile shot down America's U2 spy plane, and parents enraged as teenagers swept further into rock and roll.

As President, John F. Kennedy faced head-on a country and world in turmoil. Was Emery's charge any more or less chaotic? Sadly, every generation faces some kind of crisis. The hell of it all was, could mankind learn from their mistakes...or were they destined to repeat them? The age-old battle between good and evil raged on.

History tainting an individual for the color of their skin, their religion, or ideals didn't begin in the nineteen sixties. American Indians were forced off their land into reservations. The Civil War fought and abolished slavery. Hitler's perfect world went up in flames...but to what end...and at what cost?

Emery shook his head. How could he change the fate of the nation? Head down, he strolled across the carpet and twisted the door handle.

"Emery?"

Her voice caught him off guard. Turning, he lifted his chin to see Kathleen.

"Oh, Emery. I was so worried. Where have you been? The entire Secret Service is searching for you." She threw her arms around his neck and squeezed him close.

"In...the...shower." He squeezed her then clenched her shoulders and pressed her backward until he could gaze into her eyes. "I'm sorry I upset you, honey. I've had a lot on my mind and needed time to think, but..." A warm rush flowed down his arms and legs as he watched the fear in her face drain. "Have I ever told you how breathtakingly beautiful you are?"

The tension shadowing her face faded, and she smiled. "Perhaps, but I don't mind hearing it again."

He ran a finger over her lips. "I've missed you."

Her forehead wrinkled. "Missed me?"

"I uh...I mean...I've spent too much time worrying about the world...and not enough holding my family close. I want you to know you and the girls are the most important part of my life." He lifted her chin then ran his fingers through her hair. Drawing her close, he kissed her with the passion of ten lost years. Finally, relinquishing the kiss, he lowered his gaze to see her eyes still closed.

Slowly, she opened them. "Oh, Emery...I'm so glad you're back."

He slid his palms from her shoulders to her hands then squeezed. "I want to see the girls." He paused, considering what he needed to do as President. "Let's plan on a family dinner at six tonight. Anywhere you choose. I promise I will be there with bells on."

She tittered. "With bells on? I haven't heard that saying in years." She stared deeply into his eyes. "In fact, I don't think I've ever heard you say that...I don't know what's gotten into you this morning, but I like it."

"Good. You can expect to see a lot more of me and more of my undivided attention, too. But first, I need to let the Secret Service know I'm all right before they call out the National Guard." He took her hand and headed to the elevator.

Stepping inside, Kathleen turned to him. "I

really didn't mean to alert everyone. It's just that last night you were so concerned about the riots, anarchy, and looting. When you didn't come to bed, I—"

He placed a finger on her lips. "Shh. Last night was all on me. I should have told you I needed some peace and quiet to consider the best direction for the country."

She smiled.

When the elevator doors opened, Emery and Kathleen walked into the west wing.

The Chief of Staff's eyes went wide. "Mr. President. I thought you—"

"The announcement of my disappearance was wildly exaggerated. I'm fine. I have some important phone calls to make and work to do this morning, so I will be tied up. But can you inform the administration to be in the Cabinet Room at four p.m. for an important meeting? I'd also like to address the nation from the Oval Office tomorrow night at nine. Can you make the necessary arrangements?"

"Yes, sir," the Chief of Staff said. "Absolutely."

Emery kissed Kathleen on the cheek. "Tonight, at six?"

She smiled. "I'll text you the location."

He winked then turned and disappeared into the Oval Office.

Chapter Thirty-One

After hours of Google searches, consideration, and forethought, Emery made several phone calls, the last of which prompted him to take in a long breath before pressing Call. Thoughts churning, he steepled his fingers and pushed them against his lips. The Internet gave him many answers he needed.

Despite the prejudice Jim Rucker experienced as a youth and young adult, he spent a lifetime fighting racial injustice, educating all Americans of the divisive nature of labeling people with any generalized contentious categories, and how the term *racism* itself incited division and bred bitter hatred. Jim spear-headed programs to educate all children regardless of race, especially those focusing on charter and private schools targeting low-income neighborhoods.

For sixty years, he had dedicated his life to teaching the values he learned on that deserted island. The man was a true hero, but as Emery had sadly discovered himself, one man could only do so much.

Of course, Jim would never know Emery was the man who spent time with him on the island in 1960, and the man who met with him ten years later as a senator from the great state of Texas. Nor would Jim realize the Senator Emery Clayton—known as Clay—whose funeral he attended in 1998, was a virtual stranger. Emery wondered how much his grandfather retained of their shared memories, or of the time travel phenomenon. A soft buzz from his phone drew his attention to the present. He glanced at his watch: two-thirty. Much needed to be done before his administrative meeting.

By the time everyone gathered in the hall near the Cabinet Room, President Emery Clayton, III was already seated at the head of the table, scanning a notebook. His Cabinet secretaries and advisors entered quietly and sat around the immense mahogany table. When everyone was seated, Emery started the meeting.

"Good afternoon, ladies and gentlemen. I apologize for this morning's confusion. A lot has happened over the last twenty-four hours." *His staff actually had no idea how true that statement was.* "After hours of deliberation over the top-secret information I received yesterday, I've determined it's important you know a few details." He gazed around the table at the solemn faces. "What I'm about to reveal might shock most of you. For others, the information will shed light on the unrest our country has experienced over the last several years." He paused and glanced around the table. What he was about to say would alter the world, and no way existed to break the news easily. He drew in a lungful of air then slowly released it. "The United States is under siege…"

After rounds of whispers, President Clayton continued. "When I was elected, I vowed to heal our divided nation. But how can anyone heal what they don't understand? A silent, invisible enemy has emerged, and the nemesis slithered into our nation like viscous ooze." Again, he watched their reactions then waved a hand to calm the agitation. "Over the last decade, a virus took hold in our country and spread like a pandemic—the depth and breadth of which, was seeded, propagated, and nurtured by a power-hungry foreign government."

Ohhs and ahhs incited another round of whispers, tossing several country names into the discussion.

Secretary of State Marcus Avery leaned forward and crossed his hands on the table. "The Red Storm has been rising for years, ladies and gentlemen. This should come as no surprise." He turned toward Emery. "The question is, how deep is the dagger?"

"Secretary Avery is correct. And what better strategy than to use our weakest bond against us?"

The Secretary of Homeland Security spoke out. "Sir, what do you mean to use our weakest bond against us?"

"It's the oldest tactic in the books. Divide and conquer...primarily using what we've worked on the hardest...fought wars to correct...racial equality. Their objective...to rip apart our nation so divisively we'd never see them coming."

The Vice President leaned back into his seat. "We know they've interfered with our elections for decades."

"Under the guise of olive branches, they've taken advantage of trade relations, too," the Secretary of Commerce tossed out.

Again, Emery raised a hand, and the group silenced. "Funded by endless pockets—this one power—and a few terrorist nations—infiltrated our country...stole our technology and attacked our national treasure—our people—sowing seeds of unrest and division with suspicion, lies, hatred, malice, and fear-mongering...they even targeted our children. While we fought amongst ourselves internally, our enemies planned our defeat. Sadly, their power grab reached the pockets of key individuals within our government. Look around you. Do you notice anyone missing from our meeting?" Before continuing, he leaned back and watched as they took a mental roll call. "But those missing today only scratch the surface. Many more on the other side of the aisle took the bait as well." Emery leaned forward. "Through the years, our country has met enemies head on and won. But destroying this invisible, faceless enemy was far more difficult. Today, we rip off the mask of our enemy…and wage another World War."

Everyone sat stunned in silence, staring at each other with shock etched into their expressions.

Emery shot a nod to the Vice President, who immediately stood, walked toward the door and opened it, allowing an old man to trudge inside before closing the door again.

Pushing away from the table, Emery stood and motioned for the old man to sit at the head in his place. "I'd like to introduce a very dear friend of Senator Emery Clayton Senior—who, as you all know, was my grandfather.

The old man gazed around the table, his bushy gray eyebrows pinched together, carving a stern expression into his features.

"Mr. James Rucker stood next to and assisted Dr. Martin Luther King, Jr. many years ago and has dedicated his life to coalescing Americans through education and social relations. Before I proceed with our plan of action, Mr. Rucker has something to say I think you all should hear." Emery patted Jim's shoulder.

Jim nodded then spoke in a slow, clear, and reverent voice.

"When in the course of human events…it becomes necessary for people to dissolve political ties…and assume laws nature and God entitled to them…we

255

hold these truths to be self-evident...that all men are created equal...that they are endowed by their Creator with certain inalienable rights...that among these are life...liberty...and the pursuit of happiness."

Jim's silence held for several long beats, staring into their faces before he spoke again. "Every man, woman, and child in this country deserves the God-given birthright to equality under the Declaration of Independence regardless of color, gender, religion, race, or creed. America has survived growing pains since before the inception of the Constitution. We've fought and conquered some pretty nasty social injustices." He leaned back. "Let me tell you the story of a young, Northern black boy."

Emery smiled as he listened to the story Jim told Clay so many years ago on a remote key in the Phoenix Islands. But, when Emery heard Jim's story on the phone earlier that morning, he realized the ending was quite different from the one Clay heard. Thrilled to learn Jim lived so close by in Washington D.C., he met Clay's old friend for lunch.

James Rucker was an amazing man. He told Emery how Clay promised to let his voice be heard by the American people. Emery Clayton Senior did bring him before the Senate, but Jim feared the time wasn't right to be heard...and he was correct. Perhaps fate led Jim to a more significant destiny.

As President, Emery would finally fulfill Jim's

lifelong dream. He invited the old man to talk to the administration this afternoon…and tomorrow to the Senate and Congress. But tomorrow night, Jim's voice would finally be heard when he addressed the American people…and with any luck, his old friend would help Emery explain the war he initiated, calm the nation, and unite the country.

Jim cleared his throat then continued. "You all understand that slavery didn't originate in America, but many Americans are not aware of this. Oppression has existed since the beginning of recorded history. You're right when you say the United States is different, but not because of a vast racial divide. America is different because we've battled to purge racial division."

Emery's heart pounded as Jim spoke. How far his brother of the past had come since they parted in 1960.

"Why do you think people storm our borders to enter this country? We possess what few other countries will ever have…an unparalleled nation where we are free to discuss diverse ideas to direct a better future. That freedom and the love of our country is our strength. Our commonalities and patriotism unite us…and our diverse thoughts, creativity, ingenuity, and the right to debate differentiates America from other countries." He paused, as if waiting for his message to sink in.

"This nation is one of the least racist countries in the world." He smiled as the cabinet listened, their faces absorbed in his every word.

"There was a time when I rode a bus I had to sit in the very back. I couldn't drink from a fountain when I was thirsty or go to the bathroom when nature called unless the facilities were marked for black folks. I wasn't allowed in some restaurants and stores. Where I was allowed to buy clothes, I wasn't permitted to try them on first. The times have changed, folks. Americans are united. Of course, there will always be more to accomplish, but in today's America, people detest deplorable treatment of anyone regardless of their color or race. It's who we are as one people."

"Sadly, though, evil will always exist, lurking in the shadows to emerge when given the opportunity." He silently gazed around the room for a long moment before he continued. "There will always be some people lurking in shadows, ready to spew prejudiced vitriol when the opportunity arises. But we can deal with them one by one. Ignore their divisive banter. Give their hate no oxygen, and they'll slither back into the darkness. Those who commit racially charged crimes are criminals, and they will feel the wrath of the legal system. Hear me when I say the vast majority of Americans are fair and unbiased people at their core." Jim raised his gaze to meet Emery's.

Emery nodded reassurance for Jim to continue. Their afternoon talk was intense, and though Emery gave away no national secrets or classified information, he told Jim enough to warn the cabinet.

"Another enemy has breached our country's shore, taking aim at our heart, where we fought the hardest. They attacked our pride and tagged us as a country of racists. Intent on divide and conquer, they *prey* to see America self-destruct, so they can take our place as the strongest world power. But don't be fooled. We are not divided. As Americans, we must stand united against this enemy.

Again, he silenced for a moment and glanced around, rubbing his chin as if gaging how to proceed. "We didn't notice the threat slink into our country and strategically infiltrate our society. Once they achieved a toehold, they pushed their presence into a foothold. Covertly and slowly, they used technology and social media and transferred secrets through their consulates. They penetrated our media, our schools, and even our government. With endless wealth, they enticed key politicians in our Congress and Senate to do their bidding."

Clay folded his arms over each other and leaned against the wall, astounded at how his old friend mesmerized his audience as he wove his life story and a world of knowledge into his discourse.

"Their foothold became a stronghold...but they want more. They sowed seeds of dissent, propagandized unions, and stole the dreams of our children. Under our own noses, they hijacked America's passion, paying anarchists to subvert righteous indignation and peaceful protests—the very rights that made our nation stronger. And they paid agitators and radicals with an endless stream of money to incite riots, encourage looting, and provide fuel and fire to burn our own neighborhoods." Jim leaned back in his chair.

"Ha, what they didn't realize, though, is we noticed. They laugh in our faces, believing they've succeeded. But they've only awakened the sleeping

giant. We are Americans. Violence is not our
heritage. We can and will defeat this enemy…"

As he continued to listen, Emery smiled. He
wished he could tell Jim about his fantastic journey
through time and that Emery was the man who
befriended him all those years ago. But that couldn't
happen. What mattered now was Jim held in his
heart what Emery, as President, needed all along—
the secret weapon that would reunite the country.
When it was most needed, the passion of Jim's
dream would finally be heard.

After spending over ten years in another time,
Emery's fears no longer held him captive. The
tension drained from his muscles. Madison's
graduation meant a new beginning for his daughter,
and he'd do everything in his power to make sure
the country would be in a position to help her
dreams come true—and the dreams of every
American child regardless of their color, religion, or
creed. Emery now knew exactly what America
needed to neutralize the pockets of ignorant
intolerance and rid the nation of the fear, riots, and
anarchy plaguing the country he loved.

He was finally at peace.

Emery Clayton, III, President of the United
States of America, knew exactly what to do to save
his nation…

~ THE END ~

"It's a wonder I haven't abandoned all my ideals...
Yet I cling to them because
I still believe, in spite of everything,
that people are truly good at heart."

—Anne Frank

About the Author

USA Today & Amazon Best Selling Author, Casi McLean, pens novels to stir the soul with romance, suspense, and a sprinkle of magic. Her writing crosses genres from ethereal, captivating shorts with eerie twist endings, to believable time slips, mystical plots, and sensual romantic suspense.

Known for enchanting stories with magical description, McLean entices readers with fascinating hooks to hold them captive in storylines they can't put down. Her romance entwines strong, believable heroines with delicious, hot heroes to tempt the deepest desires, then fans the flames, sweeping readers into their innermost romantic fantasies. With suspenseful settings and lovable characters, you'll devour, you'll see, hear, and feel the magical eeriness of one fateful night. You'll swear time travel could happen, be mystified by other worldly images, and feel the heat of romantic suspense, but most of all you'll want more.

*Casi's newest series, Three Sisters Island Mysteries, is a new Lake Lanier saga presented in a cozy mystery platform. Book one, **TIMELESS SECRETS**, begins a new time slip journey revisiting a time travel portal beneath Atlanta's famous Lake Lanier. Book two, **TIMELESS TREASURES**, spins Summer and the reader back to 1692 Salem during the Salem Witch Trials. Book Three, **TIMELESS MYSTERIES,** takes Meadow on a wild ride to thwart another time traveler who want to erase Nikola Tesla from existence.

* **IN TIME FOR CHRISTMAS**— A THREE SISTERS ISLAND MAGICAL MOMENT— a unique time travel romantic suspense—a mystical, romantic Christmas story you'll never forget.

* **A SWITCH IN TIME—THE PRESIDENT IS MISSING**, is a time travel stunner where Casi teams up with her mother's never before published manuscript in a unique novel that spans sixty-years in the making-- creating a story ripped from today's headlines.

* Twins unite when a cutting-edged medical mystery merges with high-tech crime solving, creating a pulse-pounding thriller in **VIRTUALLY TIMELESS**.

* Casi's Deep State Mysteries series enters the realm of political thrillers, combined with NCIS Military and a hellastrong ghost you'll root for in **REIGN OF FIRE**, and **THE LIST— ALYSSA'S REVENGE**. Her newest work in progress, **CHINA STORM** completes the three-book series.

* Casi's signature series, Lake Lanier Mysteries, features a unique spin on romantic suspense time travel. Inspired by freak accidents, strange phenomena, and eerie lore attached to Atlanta's man-made Lake Sidney Lanier, Casi weaves together page-turning suspense and star-crossed lovers in this three-book series, **BENEATH THE LAKE, BEYOND THE MIST**, and **BETWEEN THE SHADOWS**. Toss in an almost believable time portal and Lake Lanier Mysteries will draw you in and hold you spellbound.

Find your destiny in Casi's **DESTINY COLLECTION**--five short stories with twists you'll never see coming.
myBook.to/DestinySeries

For a more personal look at Casi McLean, read her memoir, **WINGLESS BUTTERFLY—HEALING THE BROKEN CHILD WITHIN**: myBook.to/WinglessButterfly. Uniquely qualified to write self-help and inspiration, Casi tops the scale with her powerful memoir, sharing an inspirational message of courage, tenacity, and hope, while displaying her unique ability to excel in nonfiction and self-help as well as fiction.

Below you can read excerpts of Casi McLean's most popular books.
Starting with

Lake Lanier Mysteries

To give you a sneak peek of my stories, I've included book descriptions and excerpts for you. Enjoy.

Beneath the Lake Won 2019 PRG Best Time Travel Novel

2016 Best Romantic Suspense

Gayle Wilson Award of Excellence

The story was inspired by the freak accidents, strange phenomena, and eerie lore attached to Atlanta's man-made Lake Sidney Lanier.

But what if the excavation created more than a lake? What if explosions triggered a seismic shift that created a portal connecting past to future? Lake Lanier Mysteries evolved from that premise.

Time Travel, Mystery, Thriller, Romantic Suspense with Supernatural Elements.

Beneath The Lake
Book 1—Lake Lanier Mysteries

<u>Available in Print and Audible Versions</u>

A ghost town, buried beneath Atlanta's famous man-made Lake Lanier, reportedly lures victims into a watery grave. But when Lacey Montgomery's car spins out of control and hurtles into the depths of the icy water, she awakens in the arms of a stranger, in a town she's never heard of—34 years *before* she was born.

When the 2012 lawyer tangles with a 1949 hunk, fire and ice swirl into a stream of sweltering desire. Bobby Reynolds is smitten the moment the storm-ravaged woman opens her eyes and, despite adamant protest, Lacey falls in love with a town destined for extinction, and the man who vows to save his legacy.

Threatened by a nefarious stalker, the wrath of bootleggers, and twists of fate, Lacey must find the key to a mysterious portal before time rips the lovers apart, leaving their star-crossed spirits to wander forever through a ghost town buried beneath the lake.

Excerpt
Chapter 1
Lake Lanier, Georgia—June 2011

A final thud hurled him backward, flailing through brush and thickets like a rag doll. Grasping at anything to break momentum, Rob's hand clung to a branch wedged into the face of the precipice. Spiny splinters sliced his skin. Blood oozed and trickled into his palms, and one by one, his fingers slowly slipped.

A sharp crack echoed through the silence of the ravine as the bough succumbed to his weight. He plummeted into free-fall. Clenching his eyes, he drew in a deep breath, terrified of the pain, the mauling that waited on the jagged rocks below.

When icy water broke his fall, the chill kept him from losing consciousness. He spun, straining to see, but darkness enveloped him. Soggy clothing pulled him deeper—deeper into the murky, fathomless depths. He wrestled to squirm free from the waterlogged jacket dragging him down to a watery grave, watched the coat disappear into black obscurity. Panic gripped his stomach, or was it death that snaked around his chest, squeezing, squeezing, squeezing the air, the life from his body? Lack of oxygen burned his lungs, beckoning surrender, and a shard of rage pierced his gut as reality set in. He lunged upward with one last thrust and burst from the water's deadly grip, gasping for air. A gurgling howl spewed from the depths of his soul and echoed into silence.

Sunlight shimmered across a smooth, indigo lake, but aside from the slight ripples of his own paddling, nothing but stillness surrounded him.

He floated toward the shore, sucking deep breaths into his lungs until the pummeling in his chest subsided. When he reached the water's edge, he hoisted his body onto the soft red clay and collapsed while the sun's warmth drained the tension from his body.

No one knew he had survived. The rules had shifted. Now he could reinvent himself, become a stealth predator. His target: Lacey Madison Montgomery.

Beyond The Mist
Book 2—Lake Lanier Mysteries

Available in Print and Audible Versions

When a treacherous storm spirals Piper Taylor into the arms of Nick Cramer, an intriguing lawyer, she never expected to fall in love. But when he disappears, she risks her life to find him; unaware the search would thrust her into international espionage, terrorism, and the space-time continuum.

Nick leads a charmed life except when it comes to his heart. Haunted by a past relationship, he can't move forward with Piper despite the feelings she evokes. When he stumbles upon a secret portal hidden beneath Atlanta's Lake Lanier, he seizes the chance to correct his mistakes.

A slip through time has consequences beyond their wildest dreams. Can Piper find Nick and bring him home before he alters the fabric of time, or will the lovers drift forever *Beyond The Mist?*

Excerpt
Chapter 1

Lake Lanier, GA June 2012

A soft mist hovered over the moonlit lake, beckoning, luring him forward with the seductive enticement of a mermaid's song. The rhythmic clatter of a distant train moaned in harmony with a symphony of cricket chirps and croaking frogs. Mesmerized, Nick Cramer took a long breath and waded deeper into the murky cove. Dank air, laden with a scent of soggy earth and pine crawled across his bare arms. The hairs on the back of his neck bristled, shooting a prickle slithering around his spine into an icy pool quivering in the pit of his abdomen. Shots of fiery energy electrified his senses, thousands of needles spewed venom into his chest until his stomach heaved and rancid bile choked into his throat. He clenched his fingers into a tight fist, determined to fight through the fear now consuming him.

I can do this—he forged ahead—*only a few more steps and*—a sudden surge swirled around him, yanking him into a whirling vortex; a violent blue haze dragged him deeper, deeper beneath the lake into the shadowy depths. Heart pounding, he battled against the force, twisting, pulling back toward the surface with all his strength but, despite his muscular build, he spun like a feather in the wind into oblivion. When the mist dissolved, Nick Cramer had vanished.

Between The Shadows
Book 3—Lake Lanier Mysteries

Available in Print and Audible Versions

Thrust back in time, Kenzi never expected to confront deadly villains—let alone fall in love with one.

After her friend, York, encounters the ghostly image of a young woman, Mackenzie Reynolds seizes the opportunity to initiate a time jump, thrusting them back to 1865 Georgia. Resolved to thwart the girl's untimely fate, Kenzi stumbles into a deadly conflict over a stockpile of stolen Confederate gold.

An injured Civil War survivor, James Adams departs for home with a war-fatigued companion he's determined to help. After pilfering a horse and kidnapping a woman, he never dreamed his hostage would steal his heart.

Kenzi and James must unravel a deadly plot, while helping York save his ghost woman from a brutal death. But can she leave York in a violent past to save James's life?

Excerpt

"Don't you dare die on me, James Adams."

Kenzi pressed a wad of blood-soaked gauze against his abdomen. "I won't lose you. Not now."

Barely clinging to life, the man opened his eyes a slit, raised the gun still tightly gripped in his hand and shot off a round.

Stunned, she snapped around. "No." Screaming, she dove for the barrel through a hazy blue mist.

Again, the gun rang out as the patient fell unconscious.

"Help. Someone, please help".

A muted voice murmured from beyond the fog. "Dr. Reynolds? Is that you?"

Her frantic reply cried out, "Yes, of course it's me. Hurry. He's bleeding out."

"Brady..." James's voice faded as he slipped into semiconscious mumbling.

Yanking the pistol from his grip with her right hand, she maintained pressure with her left. A heartbeat later, the cylinder encasing them rotated open. Kenzi stood then sprinted across the room past an attendant then pounded on a fist-sized alert button affixed to the wall. The resulting alarm shrieked through the underground chamber, reverberating as it radiated throughout the compound. A second man dressed in a white jumpsuit burst through double doors.

"Gurney. Now." Kenzi screamed at both attendants. "And O-Neg blood. Hurry. Go, go, go." She ran to James and knelt beside him. Lifting his head, she slid a knee underneath it for support and smoothed a chunk of his dark brown hair from his face. "I've sacrificed way too much to have you die now," she whispered. "My ass will burn for this. Not to mention the repercussions for abandoning York."

Pulse racing, she checked his bandage. Despite her efforts, streams of crimson still oozed from the wound. Pressing again on the gauze, she shook her head. "Oh God. I have no idea what blood type you are, but you should tolerate O-negative." She pressed harder on his wound. "Jesus help you, James. You've lost so much blood. Just please, hang on."

Again, the double doors swung wide. This time, a gurney pushed through, followed by the two men. One ran to Kenzi's side.

"Help me lift him." Her hands, slick with blood, shot to her white T-top, already drenched in crimson. On a second thought, she swept them down the rear of her jeans. Then, sliding her slippery arms beneath his back, she braced her stance with one bent knee.

"One, two, three." They heaved him in tandem onto the gurney. She snatched a bottle of Betadine from the attached supply basket and doused her hands then splashed more on James's forearm, grasped an IV and punctured a vein on the inside of his wrist with the sterile needle. Once connected, she hooked the blood pouch on the IV pole and barked at the team, "Let's move. If this man bleeds out, there will be hell to pay."

The men, poised with hands on the side of the rails, awaited their next move. "Where to, Dr. Reynolds?"

Kenzi stared at James's ashen face, worried her meager experience wasn't enough to save his life—but she had no option. "Surgery."

Springing into action, one man rolled the gurney down the hallway, while a second leapt onto the base and slipped an oxygen mask over James's nose and mouth. "I hope this guy isn't allergic to Propofol." He attached an anesthesia drip to the IV. "Judas Priest. What happened to him to cause such a gaping wound?"

"He was shot...with a musket."

Deep State Mysteries
<u>Reign of Fire</u>
Book 1—Deep State Mysteries

<u>Available in Print and Audible Versions</u>

To expose a faction threatening America's democracy, Emily Rose joins forces with a team investigating her sister's murder, but she never expects to fall in love—or to encounter her twin's ghost.

Ashton Frasier accepts his detective career choice means a life of bachelorhood—until Emily Rose blows into his world.

Surrounded by danger with the country's democracy at stake, Emily and Ash must protect the White House while taming their mysterious burning passion—lit by cunning spirit with good intentions.

Can a ghost spark love in the midst of chaos?

Excerpt
Chapter One

Alyssa Rose shifted her gaze in every direction, searching for suspicious bystanders. Her cloak-and-dagger cover had her exit the Capitol through the door next to the ladies' room. The out-of-character detour might have been an insignificant detail, but evading possible surveillance made her breathe easier. Walking east of the Capitol altered her routine, so a side trip to this particular mail drop provided a prime spot to send her letter under the radar.

Trembling as she approached her destination, she scrutinized everyone, zeroing in on their eyes. If she observed someone with a shifty gaze or noticed an unusual glance in her direction, she'd walk past the postal box and circle back later. No one could see her mail this letter.

Taking a deep breath, she slid the envelope from beneath her coat, ran her finger across the address then quickly slipped the letter into the mailbox at the corner of Independence and Pennsylvania. A cold chill slithered around her neck, shooting pins and needles in every direction before tightening the knot already twisting in her stomach. Drawing together the lapels of her royal-blue coat, she snatched the soft cashmere and cast one more glance around before striding across Pennsylvania toward 2nd Street.

The icy tingle numbing Alyssa to the bone had little to do with the cool March weather. The crisp air might have exacerbated the sensation, but her accidental discovery initiated the anxiety, and she couldn't erase the images seared into her mind. If anyone discovered what she saw, her very life would be in jeopardy. God, she wished she could un-know what now dominated her thoughts.

Only a few weeks ago, Alyssa lived a blissful life of naiveté. Her family reared her to hold dear the advantages her country bestowed, and when her senior field trip took the class to Williamsburg, Virginia, she experienced a strong sense of patriotism that continued to blossom.

Wyatt, her brother, fanned the fire blazing in her belly. Despite his horrendous accident in Afghanistan, his love for country burned eternal. If anything, the explosion that took his legs fanned the flames, and he encouraged Alyssa to use her skills to fight for a better country from within the body that created the laws. An intern job would help her learn policy to springboard to a political profession and open doors where she could make a real difference.

She worked her butt off long and hard to secure a spot in this program. A budding Intern for Congressman Derek Winfield, Alyssa saw this job as her big chance. Granted, the position seemed mundane, if not ridiculous. She simply walked in, picked up a pile of messages and dispersed them to offices on The Hill accordingly.

Email would have been a lot easier and faster. At first, she thought the task was a newbie-only job assigned to interns, forcing them to learn the lay of the land. But Derek explained email messages were traceable. They were etched into hard drives and nearly impossible to erase.

So, for the time being interoffice mail delivery was her job and a rung of the ladder she'd be happy to pass on when the time came. Until then, she didn't mind starting her career at the bottom rung of the ladder. The mailroom had its perks. Playing courier allowed her to walk historic streets and take in the ambiance, imagining the town during different eras and all the presidents who once strolled on antiquated roads beneath her.

Her innocent walks around Capitol Hill mingled business with pleasure. Ear buds firmly tucked in place, she listened to her favorite mix, while chalking up her health goal of ten thousand-steps. The bustle between L'Enfant Plaza and the Capitol energized her. Wide-eyed, she relished the inspiration America's forefathers instilled—until the dreadful day an arbitrary Starbucks patron collided with her as he bolted into the store. Memories swirling, her mind replayed the fateful day in a 24/7 constant loop. How could such an innocent random event spiral into this very real nightmare?

Purse slung over her shoulder, with a tray of coffee orders in one hand and a stack of to-be-delivered messages in the other, Alyssa had no control as her balancing act flew into the air, leaving a deluge of coffee-splattered, mocha-scented letters cluttering the entrance. "No, no, no." After flinging her hands, she snatched a pile of napkins and frowned at the mess surrounding her. She drew in a deep breath. Indignation seething inside, she clenched a fist to repress her reaction to a simmer.

"Son of a bitch." The dark-haired man's attention dropped to his camelhair coat. Brushing off coffee beads to keep them from soaking into his lapel, he flashed a gaze toward Alyssa, offering a lame apology. "Sorry. This mess is totally on me."

A tinge of satisfaction befell her, as she eyed his splattered attire. "I can see that." She chuckled.

He followed her line of vision and glanced downward. "Perfect." Grabbing more napkins, he cleaned whipped cream from his shoes then wiped his pants before noticing a sizable blotch on the pocket of his camelhair. "Damn it." Tugging off the coat, he draped it across the side of the condiment stand and reached for an arbitrary towel clumped into a mound beside him, then pressed on the stain. Not until he appeared to be satisfied with his own results, did he return his attention to Alyssa, now squatting beside him, cleaning the coffee puddle. "Here, let me help you."

She rolled her eyes but said nothing, although her thoughts rebuked him. *It's about damn time you focused on the chaos you caused...*

The stranger knelt with towel in hand and sloshed it around in the pool of coffee, making the mess exponentially worse, while Alyssa fought to keep her boiling frustration at bay. Shifting her gaze to her scattered and smothered envelopes, she turned and duck-walked, gathering them into a drenched pile. She clenched her jaw, then shook and examined each packet, an effort that did little more to minimize the damage than changing splotches to dribbles.

When an attendant came to the rescue and began mopping the floor, the stranger stood, retrieved his coat, and draped it over an arm. "Damn. Can this day get any worse?" He glanced at his watch. "Son of a—now, I'm running late." Turning toward Alyssa, he reached into his back pocket and drew out a business card then handed it to her. "Take this. I'll pay your dry-cleaning bill. Just shoot me an email." Instead of buying a coffee, he smacked open the door and rushed outside, quickly disappearing into the busy crowd.

Alyssa's last nerve had her grinding her teeth as she inspected her own coat for stains. Surprised her clothing escaped the coffee cascade, she stuffed the man's proffer into her pocket without even glancing at his name. She felt a bit atoned that the bulk of the mess splashed over him as opposed to her. But a quick glance at her letters doused the brief restitution. Again, she blotted the notes in her charge in an attempt to salvage them, hoping the incident wouldn't cost her job.

When the attendant finished mopping the floor, he asked if he could remake her order.

Alyssa nodded and thanked him, still wiping her mess. Why did the collision have to happen to her? She cussed the arrogant man under her breath. How dare he blow her off after causing the incident?

Instead of the attendant, a manager returned to the scene with a carryout tray of fresh coffee. "This batch is on the house. I saw that whole scenario go down." He shook his head. "That guy could have at least helped you with your mail, since he was the reason your envelopes were soiled."

"Thank you so much." Alyssa appreciatively took the order. "I'm sorry to make such a mess."

The manager shrugged. "Hey, you did nothing wrong. No worries. Stuff happens."

"Tell that to my boss." Rolling her eyes, Alyssa splayed the pile of notes in her hand. "How can I deliver these to senators and congressmen?" Heat raged in her cheeks. She squeezed her eyes shut for a long beat, resisting the march of berating anger clenching her stomach. True, the accident wasn't her fault, but if she hadn't been so engrossed in listening to her music, she might have seen the man busting through the door and avoided the mishap altogether.

The manager smiled and raised an eyebrow. "The damage looks superficial. Maybe you could just replace the envelopes?" He gazed at the soggy array. "Look, the coffee didn't stain the addresses beyond recognition, and I doubt the damage seeped through to the inside messages."

"Perhaps…" Alyssa's frown faded as she inspected the notes and considered his idea.

"You might be right. Thanks." If she hurried to her office and simply switched the envelopes, she could deliver the messages with only a slight delay…no one would be the wiser. Gathering her paperwork and coffee, she rushed outside then scurried to her office, assured the plan just might save her ass.

In theory, the switch was a no-brainer. She never dreamed one instinctual *cover-your-ass* choice could threaten her life. Opening the coffee-stained envelopes and switching the notes to identical, deliverable packets seemed the perfect solution—until she discovered the one note never intended for delivery…the note that validated the existence of a shadow government.

Geez, if only she hadn't opened that wretched letter. She gasped the moment she saw an immediate burn order splashed in red across the top of the page above a simple title: The List. As she read on, she swallowed hard, her breath catching in her throat. She had no idea how deep the faction went, or which treasonous federal officials would be revealed once the list was decoded.

Racking her brain, she couldn't recall where the delivery had come from. She couldn't remember picking it up from any of the offices. But she had to admit her mindless deliveries rarely demanded her undivided attention. Still, the envelope was smaller than the others, and it didn't carry the standard Federal Government insignia.

A loud honking from a car speeding through the traffic signal brought her thoughts back to the moment. *Dear God.* The last thing she needed was a jolt to boost her adrenaline.

Biting the edge of her bottom lip, Alyssa shoved her trembling hands into her pockets and picked up her pace, rationalizing her decision. She didn't intend to snoop that day. She simply couldn't deliver soggy, damaged mail and expect no one would notice. An entry-level job meant no demotions existed. If she didn't perform up to expectations, firing was the only alternative. Her priority...she had to save her dream-job.

Slowing her pace, she entered the Capitol Rotunda and gazed at the vast marvel surrounding her. How did her dream morph into the nightmare now clenching her throat in a stranglehold...a nightmare from which she couldn't awaken? She shuddered. Not in her wildest dreams had she ever expected the politicized bureaucrats and pundits on Capitol Hill would swallow her whole.

Discovering an encrypted list had her bursting at the seams to tell someone. How could she simply ignore the message and let the powers that be sweep their dirty little secrets under a politicized rug? But who could she turn to or believe in enough to provide solid advice? Anyone could be involved in this "Association." For weeks, trust no one had been her mantra. But each passing day had her more convinced someone lurked in the shadows, watching her every move, and the paranoia smothered her with feelings of impending doom.

Fiddling with the locket around her neck, she thought about her twin...the only person Alyssa truly trusted, aside from her brother. Emily had a sixth sense that seemed to guide her decisions. She would know whether to pass along the secret list or burn it.

Several times over the last three weeks, Alyssa started to call Emily, and each time she stopped short of pushing Send. Derek taught his intern well. If "The Association" tailed Alyssa, her phone would likely be bugged, too. The thought of putting her twin in danger clamped Alyssa's stomach like a coiling snake squeezing until she couldn't breathe. A letter sent from a random mail drop would go undetected. She'd wait until the two could meet. In the meantime, Alyssa would lay low, do her job, and avoid confrontation.

Glancing at her watch, she realized the late hour. Another workday drew to an end, and she'd need to rush if she wanted to catch her train home. Exiting at the rear of the Capitol Rotunda, she again tightened the grasp on her coat collar, wishing she'd remembered to grab the blue and white scarf she usually wore on windy mornings. The chill within her deepened as she strode the same route, she had walked every day for the past year. West on Independence to the L'Enfant Plaza Metro Station where she caught the Silver train line to McLean, Virginia. From there, she drove home.

Arriving just in time to catch her shuttle, she drew in a deep breath and stepped from the platform into the train. When the door closed, she squeezed her eyes tightly then released the pressure to relax the pinch twisting in the back of her neck. Once she knew Emily received her message, Alyssa felt sure together they could devise a plan to end her nightmare. She leaned back in her seat deep in thought, feeling thankful she survived another day—looking past a dark, hooded figure hunched only a few seats away.

The List—Alyssa's Revenge
Book 2—Deep State Mysteries

Print and Audible Versions Available

Description

USA Today Bestselling Author, Casi McLean's new Deep State Mystery, The List—Alyssa's Revenge, is a fast paced, cross-genre novel that combines supernatural, romantic suspense, and an NCIS mystery into a stunning thriller. Evil oozes from the pages as she takes us on an incredible journey through the underbelly of society.

When her fiancé is injured in Afghanistan, Harper Drake immerses herself in her military career. Now, as NCIS Director, she heads a secret faction, fighting corruption and terrorism—until she's abducted by a trafficking cartel.

Wyatt Rose can't overcome his loss—especially after his sister's murder. When the New Patriots recruit him, he finds a traumatized girl that spirals him down a rabbit hole of conspiracy, drug smugglers, and slavery.

Obsessed with revenge, can a ghost save Wyatt and Harper before her rage explodes, or will she spin them all through the gates of Hell?

When Revenge Sparks Danger — Karma is Hell!

★★★★★ "So many twists and subplots pepper this suspense, but they all come together into a tapestry of amazing imagination and powerful writing! Casi McLean has pulled off another genre bending tale that will draw readers in like bees to honey!" —ToMeTender Book Blog Reviews

★★★★★ "Casi McLean takes us on an incredible journey through the underbelly of society… [the reality of] a fifteen-year-old caught in the web of human trafficking… and a supernatural element I couldn't put down."— N.N. Light's Book Heaven

Excerpt
Chapter One

Hearing the doorlatch click closed, Hanna slid the handcuffs off her thin wrists, stood, then tiptoed across the cold, cement floor. She peered through the cracked window and saw him drive away.
"Is Damien gone?"

Hanna nodded then turned toward the voice.

"It's dark so make sure he's not testing us again." The young girl, still shackled to a plumbing pipe under the sink, trembled. She drew her knees to her chest then wrapped her free arm around them.

Hanna wiped a tear from her cheek, scooted across the concrete floor then knelt beside her. Yanking at the child's handcuffs, she whispered, "I don't want to leave you here."

Sarah forced a haggard smile. No longer did her eyes sparkle with the innocence of a thirteen-year-old child. Like windows into her shattered soul, her gaze seemed cold and hollow.

Hanna's heart broke every time she thought of the abuse Sarah had already survived.

When her family moved to El Paso, Texas, Sarah's shy nature left her feeling like an outsider. Her super social parents never understood why Sarah had difficulty making friends. "It's easy, Sarah. Just put yourself out there. Talk to people," her mother advised. But Sarah didn't know what to say...until Dylan caught up to her walking home one afternoon. An older boy paying attention to Sarah delighted her. Finally, someone noticed her, talked to and made her feel normal. Thrilled at the changes they saw in their daughter, her parents encouraged the friendship.

Every weekday before school, Dylan met her at the street corner and walked her to class and each afternoon he'd escort her home. Over

the next few months, he charmed her, gave her thoughtful gifts, told her how beautiful she was—
—and said he loved her. On her birthday, he invited her to a concert at The Plaza Theater. Sarah was over the moon...but her parents weren't.

The extravagant venue made them suspicious of Dylan's intentions. After a shower of questions turned into a huge fight—resulting in a month's restriction and forbidding her from seeing Dylan—Sarah texted him, snuck out that night—and her life spun into Hell. Dylan delivered her to Diablo. Betrayed and terrified, she watched as the slave-trader dealt him $1,000 cash.

Smiling, Dylan winked. "Thanks, kiddo." Then he turned and strolled away, counting his stash.

Though Diablo held her captive for a week as they drove to Atlanta, he didn't harm her. She ate well, received nice clothes, and he never laid a hand on her.

"A lot of big-spenders will come for the Super Bowl. A blonde-haired, blue-eyed beauty like you will easily bring in $400 or more for a half hours work." He rubbed his hands together. "And a hefty profit for me." He chuckled.

Hanna had heard a similar hype from Damien, but her abduction wasn't quite as elaborately calculated...

A Note to the Reader

A personal request:

If you enjoyed this story, please consider posting a review on Amazon, Bookbub and Goodreads. Reviews are the lifeblood of an author's world, and I cherish each one. From the bottom of my heart, thank you for your support!

YOU are my inspiration.
Your friendship and support is priceless!

Casi McLean